A mother will do anything to obtain justice for her child.

After crashing a holiday party, Samantha Wycoff slips away to the restroom where she stares at her reflection and wonders, "How the hell did I get here?"

Six months earlier, her son, Thomas, was beaten so severely he did not recover. Samantha knows his girlfriend, Velvet Flores, is guilty, but with no witnesses and what Samantha knows is a fake alibi, the police and courts can do nothing.

Micah Kerrick, Thomas's childhood best friend, offers to help her, but only if she'll join his team of government troubleshooters. A retired schoolteacher slash church lady slash professional volunteer would be the perfect cover for any mission – except one.

Will Samantha agree to a career change and join Micah's Misfits? Will Micah's handler allow such an unusual agreement to stand? Or will Samantha find herself facing certain termination?

Copyright © 2021 by Cooper McKenzie

First Publication: June 2021

Cover design by Scott Carpenter

Editing by Red Quill Editing, LLC

Cooper McKenzie, LLC

1302 Ascot Street

Georgetown, TX 78626

Print ISBN 978-14-7372817-0-2

Least Likely Suspect

Revenge

Cooper McKenzie

DEDICATION

For Miss Honey, the Diva Dog, the Princess Fuzzybutt. Some days you are the only reason I get up in the morning when I would rather lie in bed and hide from the world.

Special thanks to Beth DiLoreto for her encouragement in finishing.

PROLOGUE

December 18th – The Present

I wandered the room carrying a delicate crystal wineglass half-full of ginger ale without ice, half afraid someone would call me out as an interloper. I knew only one person at the combination birthday and Christmas party, and he, too, was there without an invitation from either the hosts or the caterers.

It took concentration to keep my expression pleasantly neutral as I wandered the room, moving from group to group, lingering at each only a few minutes before moving to the next.

I spent more time studying the Christmas decorations than I did interacting with my fellow guests. The Christmas decorations were so overdone it looked like Techno-Santa had moved in for the season. Seven twinkling ten-foot tall artificial gold Christmas trees with a rainbow of glass ornaments and ropes of red and green blinking lights filled the large first floor living room. The trees glittered nearly as brightly as the female party guests in their sequined-covered designer dresses and silver and gold and diamond jewelry. The men in their black, designer label tuxedos provided a sedate balance to the overblown feminine sparkles.

Moving to a quiet corner, I eased my way into a small alcove between the largest of the Christmas trees and the wall. I used the wall for balance as I kicked off my right shoe. Closing my eyes, I fought down a moan as I massaged my sore tootsies. I clenched my teeth as I put the right shoe back on and took off the left, repeating the massage. Once my shoes were back in place, I pulled my smartphone from the hidden pocket in my skirt and checked the time. Eight twenty-eight. Seventeen minutes until Micah would make contact.

It took a few seconds to regain my balance and deal with the pain of wearing the unfamiliar four-inch stiletto heels. I normally wore walking shoes and clogs. Taking a deep breath, I forced my facial muscles back into an expression both pleasant yet aloof. Once I felt I'd mastered that, I stepped out from behind the tree and rejoined the party.

As I moved around the room for the third time, I smiled and returned greetings appropriate for the evening and the holiday season. I listened with a small town woman's naïveté to the conversations that ranged from international business deals, which would be finalized after the first of the year, to the hot gossip surrounding the latest in what was apparently a long line of much younger men the now 55-year-old birthday girl was banging. Living a small, conservative, conventional life, this party was quite enlightening as to the lives of the uber-upper class of movers and shakers who lived inside the Capital Beltway.

What surprised me most was no one questioned my presence. I had been certain a woman no one knew, wearing a plain black, no-designer-label dress and shoes bought off the rack at the Potomac Mills outlet mall that afternoon would be questioned.

Micah had assured me these people were too self-involved to ask about yet another stranger in a room full of strangers; nevertheless, I had doubted him. Needing to cover my ass in case I was questioned, we had worked up a story that would put off even the most determined gossip. I even had an excuse for the elbow-length black lace gloves I wore with the simple, cap-sleeve, floor-length black dress.

"Canapé?" A familiar voice asked softly as a tray nearly full of beautifully displayed nibbles floated into view before me.

Looking up into the deep blue eyes of Micah Kerrick, I breathed my first easy breath since walking in the front door. My ass, back, and every other part of me was now covered.

I had to fight the nearly overwhelming urge to throw myself into his arms and beg him to take me away to somewhere that did not smell of canned pine scent mixed with a couple dozen designer perfumes, all of which made my nose itch. But this was why I was here. This was my test. This was what I'd signed on for. I would be the last one suspected of any nefarious deeds in any room with more than three people in it.

And that's why Micah had agreed to bring me on this mission.

This is for Thomas, I reminded myself silently.

Instead of dragging Micah and his tray of goodies down the hall to the first empty room we could find, I raised my glass and took a sip as I studied the tray he held before me. Each bite-sized morsel was nestled perfectly in its own gold foil paper cup.

"What are they?" I murmured just loud enough for him to hear.

"Salmon puffs and crab stuffed mushroom caps," he answered softly. He lowered his voice even further. "These are better than the other stuff they're offering."

I chose the smallest of the mushrooms and, after popping it whole into my mouth, placed the foil back on the tray. As I chewed, I had to work to keep my expression neutral and not pull a face. The too-vinegary taste assaulted my palate. The vinegar overshadowed any hint of crab, spice, and whatever else might have been in the mix. Compared to these people, I was a country bumpkin, but back home in North Carolina, this kind of appetizer would be served straight from the oven without anything but crabmeat, Italian-seasoned breadcrumbs, and Parmesan cheese in the stuffing.

I forced myself to finish chewing before I swallowed, draining my drink to get it down. Barely.

"Different," I remarked wryly with a smirk.

Micah smiled in understanding as our eyes met. So much assurance conveyed in his gaze, which lasted only a few seconds, before he murmured, "Upstairs to the right. First door is the bathroom. Top shelf of the linen closet. I'll be there in ten."

I nodded as he moved away. Searching for an open powder room and curiosity about the rest of the house's Christmas decorations was the story I would use should anyone stop me.

I worked my way out of the living room to the entry hall and up the stairs, admiring pictures and decorations as I went. I began to take slow deep breaths as nerves began to knot my gut up. Maybe eating the mushroom cap had been a mistake. The next half hour would be stressful enough, without the possibility of getting sick from a hoity-toity, crappy crab stuffing that should have been trashed ... after the chef had been forced to eat three or four himself.

At the top of the staircase, I turned right and found the bathroom. It was hard to miss. It was the only room with an open door, and the overhead light shown bright. Stepping through the doorway, I quickly closed the door and twisted the lock. Only then did I take a semi-relaxed breath.

Opening the linen closet door, I stood on tiptoes and slid my hand under the pile of white towels on the top shelf. I stretched and patted until I felt the pouch I needed, which was several inches back from the edge of the shelf. Holding onto a lower shelf, I stretched myself another inch and caught the pouch between two fingertips. It took too long to pull the pouch free of the towels hiding it while trying not to pull the stack of linens down on top of me.

It felt like it took forever, but I finally extracted the pouch. After patting the fluffy towels back into place, I closed the door and moved to the counter across the room. The double sinks left little space to work, but my entire life, and especially these last few months, had taught me to be adaptable. Unzipping the pouch, I confirmed the contents before placing it in the sink on my right. I reached down and pulled my skirt up. It took only a few seconds to work the pieces of the snub-nosed ceramic rifle with its built-in scope free from the two red satin garters holding it strapped securely along the inside of my left thigh.

Another minute ticked by too fast as I retrieved the metal firing mechanism from the pouch, and added it to the rifle. This turned the otherwise inanimate object into a powerful and highly illegal killing machine. I pulled out the two small, special darts Domingo had fashioned especially for this evening from the small brown plastic pharmacy prescription bottle also included in the pouch and slid them into the rifle's breech before closing it with a solid snap. Slipping the pouch under the bottom garter, I smoothed the skirt of my dress back into place.

I caught my reflection in the mirror and met eyes that, once upon a time, had sparkled with an innocent joy for life. Tonight, thanks to colored contacts, they appeared a dark green instead of the milk chocolate brown they had been since childhood. The light auburn, shoulder-length wig made me appear fashionably pale, which the carefully applied makeup emphasized. I barely recognized myself, but being unrecognizable as myself was the idea. Change enough of my appearance to keep me from being caught and questioned once the mission was completed.

My gaze dropped to take in the rest of my Rubenesque appearance. The dress molded to my full breasts and rounded belly. Not as much as it would have six months before, but there was still quite a bit of work to do if I wanted to appear as sleek and svelte as the women downstairs.

Raising my gaze to my eyes once more, I asked the polished, sophisticated-appearing woman in the mirror the question that had been burning in my brain since I walked in the front door an hour ago. "How the hell did I get here?"

Chapter One

Six months earlier – The Past

Would anyone even miss me? I thought as I stared across the mile-wide, flat, black void stretching out before me. The Neuse River ran silent and dark through eastern North Carolina, separating New Bern from the small community of Bridgeton on the other side.

Hell, how long would it be before someone realized I was no longer around?

A day?

A week?

Longer?

Would my neighbors miss seeing me quick march by their house each morning? Would my Facebook friends notice my absence? Or would they assure one another I was fine and had gone silent as we all do once in a while when the cyberworld becomes too intrusive on real life?

Except for Thomas, even what was left of my family wouldn't make a fuss for months, if then. Thomas might check on me, but only because he would need money, food, or a place to crash while he and Velvet took some time apart. Again.

Staring into the flat blackness of the river, I released the sadness overflowing my heart and soul through my tear ducts. I did not bother to wipe away the tears filling my eyes and rolling in hot trails down my wind-chilled cheeks.

Over the past few months, I had pleaded with God to bring a new reason to live into my life. Preferably a man who would hug me long enough and tight enough for all the broken pieces of my heart to fuse back together. Someone who would witness the rest of my days so my eventual passing would not go unnoticed.

Since my husband, Jarrod, died three years ago, I had fulfilled the few childhood dreams my fears and small-town mentality had not destroyed.

I had already lived decades longer than I had ever expected to. The politically tense era during the seventies and eighties when I was growing up had been such that I had never expected to reach my thirtieth year, much less my fifty-fourth.

Yet here I stood, as lost and rudderless as I had felt that long ago June evening when I graduated from high school oh so many years ago. Funny thing was, people still told me the world lay at my feet, and I could do anything I wanted; all I had to do was do it. Problem was, I had no idea where to chart my future's course. As a middle-aged woman, I had as much life ahead of me as I had behind.

I had lived my life without ever making long-range plans. I moved through each day, becoming a schoolteacher because it was something I enjoyed, and the job paid enough to help keep the financial ends meeting. I had spent my life so focused on keeping the family's financial nose above water that decades had passed in the blink of an eye with little to show for my efforts.

My marriage of twenty years ended with my husband's death after a short, intense bout of lung cancer the doctors had been hard pressed to identify until it was too late to slow, much less cure. Our son Thomas was not speaking to me at that moment because I refused to finance the self-indulgent life he felt he should not have to work for. During his teen years, I was certain he would end up in jail, or worse, but so far, he had surprised me. It had taken time, but he had grown into a man who, sometimes, seemed wiser and more mature than I was.

At least, until his latest girlfriend swept him off his feet.

After meeting Velvet Flores for the first time, I once again wondered why Thomas made some of his life choices. There were times I felt like his brain had simply turned off for those critical few seconds of the decision-making process. Velvet Flores was one of those times, even though he claimed to love her.

My biggest concerns were about how she treated my son like a sugar daddy, demanding he spend money on her he did not have. During their time together, she had caused the current rift between us that I could not see a way to repair. I refused to support this lifestyle she, and by extension, he wanted, and at twenty-four, he was bound and determined to show me and the world he knew what he was doing by staying with this woman.

My friends, some of whom I had known for decades, had their own lives, their own families, their own interests. Everyone was busy with the job of living.

Everyone, it seemed, but me.

I stared at the three-foot high metal spike fence, the only thing separating me from the mile-wide Neuse River. I glanced to my right, down the length of fence, which ended at the very corner of the park where the Trent River flowed into the Neuse before flowing southeastward into the Pamlico Sound and ultimately the Atlantic Ocean. All I had to do was walk the handful of yards to the open space and throw myself into the gaping black void of river.

Once again, the fears that had plagued me all my life held me frozen where I stood. Fear of what is on the other side of the veil that hung between life and death. Fear of what comes after the heart stops beating, the blood stills, and the soul is no longer bound to the body.

Fear of never finding my place in this world or the next.

Would I enter heaven and find myself enfolded in Father God's loving arms? Or end up in the fires of the other side? Or on some plane of limbo in between because I had committed suicide?

Before I could make the final decision and act upon it, my cellphone shivered in my pocket a second before it rang out, sounding like the telephones of my childhood that hung on the kitchen wall and had to be connected to a separate machine to take messages in case you missed the call. Pulling the phone from my pocket, I checked the screen.

The number was local, but not one I recognized. My well-developed sixth sense screamed at me I *needed* to take the call. Instead of silencing the phone as I normally would, I slid my finger across the screen and answered.

"Hello?" I queried, half expecting the caller to hang up when they heard a middle-aged woman on the other end. It would not be the first time I had gotten a hang-up or sorry-wrong-number call. The other option was a recording wanting to discuss renewing the nonexistent warranty on my car.

But the caller did not hang up. "Who is this, please?" A male voice asked, sounding serious and official.

The ice-cold shivery premonition of bad news about to come snaked its way down my spine at the same time my scalp tingled.

"Who were you calling?" I asked in return suspiciously.

I was just paranoid enough and experienced enough to know kooks called at all hours of the day and night, and it was, after all, nearly midnight on a Tuesday in June. Hardly the time to be receiving a happy phone call.

"Ma'am, I'm Sergeant Lewis Benson of the New Bern Police Department. I'm calling about a Thomas Wycoff. This was the number he had listed in his phone as his emergency contact."

"Oh, yes. I'm his mother, Samantha Wycoff. Has something happened to Thomas?"

My self-absorbed depressive state receded with a nearly audible whoosh. Thomas was in trouble. The mother genes kicked in as my heartbeat picked up its pace. I turned from the water and began walking across the grass toward the only vehicle in the empty park, my four-year-old white Jeep Wrangler four-door. My heart began to pound as my mind raced through the possibilities, always coming back to the most obvious.

Before Sergeant Benson could answer my last question, I asked the next questions that immediately came to mind. "What did she do to him? It wasn't drugs was it? Will Thomas be hospitalized locally or sent to Greenville? Will he be all right?"

"Ma'am, your son was severely beaten this evening and is on his way to the emergency room here in New Bern. The doctors there will determine whether he can be treated locally or needs to be transferred to the trauma center in Greenville."

"Can you tell me what happened?" I asked as I pressed the unlock button on my key fob. Climbing in, I took second to activate the phone's speaker and set the phone on the dashboard. I tapped the automatic lock button on the door with one hand while I slid the key into the ignition with the other. I pulled my seatbelt across my middle and clicked it into place, and finished preparing to drive.

"Several neighbors called nine-one-one after hearing a loud argument coming from your son's residence. By the time I arrived on the scene and found your son, whoever had been screaming at him and, apparently, beating him was gone."

"She calls herself Velvet Flores, but I'm not sure if that's her real name or not," I said before he could ask his next question. "She lives there with my son and works at one of the country clubs in town as a waitress. I'm not sure which one because she changes jobs every couple of months. Now, if you don't mind, I need to get to the hospital."

"Yes, ma'am. I'll see you there," he managed to say before I cut the connection and dropped the phone into the exterior pocket of my purse. I turned the key and headed out of the park as fast as I could, ignoring the ten mile per hour speed limit signs.

CHAPTER TWO

It took every bit of concentration to drive halfway across town to the hospital without speeding or running any of the dozen or so traffic lights as I drove up Front Street, around the traffic circle, down Broad Street and up Neuse Boulevard to the hospital. Though I was the only car on the road, I gritted my teeth to keep from driving more than five miles per hour over the speed limit. I was, after all, a law-abiding church lady.

As I drove, I began to make a mental list of calls I would need to make and what would need to be done once the doctors figured out what was going on with Thomas. This was not the first time Velvet had taken her frustrations out on my son, but I was determined it would be the last. One way or another, Thomas would not be returning to live with the animal who had put him in the hospital twice before in the eight months they had been dating. If nothing else, I would bring him home with me, and he would stay in his old room until he got on his feet again.

Parking in the nearly empty parking lot, I pressed the door lock as I climbed out. I slammed the door closed and race-walked toward the west end of the building where the emergency room lights glowed brightly. Outside the sliding doors, I stopped for a moment to catch my breath. At the same time, I once again admitted to myself it was way past time to get back into shape. Being a couch potato might be fine, but I needed to start exercising beyond just my daily walk around the neighborhood. For a split second it occurred to me that the mind went off in weird directions when under extreme stress.

Once I caught my breath, I moved toward the automatic door and waited for it to slowly slide open. As I entered, the citrusy antiseptic smell slammed me in the face. My nose twitched and my sinuses began to bog up. Rubbing my nose to keep from sneezing, I entered the second set of doors before crossing to the information desk. I was so focused on getting to Thomas it took a second to register the otherwise empty waiting room.

The clerk looked like she was having a hard time staying awake. "I'm here about Thomas Wycoff."

"Are you family?" she asked as she typed into her computer. This was one of those times I was glad computers had been invented, though most of the time, I could care less about the latest developments in modern technology.

"I'm his mother."

"He's been moved into surgery," the clerk clicked a few more keys. "You won't be able to see him until afterward, but you can wait in the surgical waiting room until then, if you'd like."

"How do I get there?"

"Go through that door and take the second hall to the left. When you reach the main hallway take a right and it will be down a ways on your left," the clerk recited automatically.

"Thank you," I said before heading to the door she had indicated.

As I approached, the door buzzed and opened when I pulled on the handle. Stepping through, I did not wait for it to click closed again, but hurried forward. I recited the directions under my breath as I quick marched down the hall. By the time I found the door to the surgical waiting room, my out-of-shape legs were yelling for a respite.

Stepping inside, I shivered as cold air blew down from a ceiling vent. After identifying myself to the clerk manning the information desk here, I practically begged for information on Thomas, especially what had happened to him and the extent of his injuries.

Going to the computer, the woman called up his file. She recited the same information the clerk in the ER had given me, in the same flat, bored tone of voice. Thomas was in critical condition and being prepared for surgery. Other than that, the clerk refused to say anything further.

"If you'd like, I can call back and let them know you're here. They'll send someone out to fill you in on what's happening, and the doctors can come out and talk to you once they've finished."

"Thank you, that would be wonderful," I nodded and a forced smile.

While the clerk made her phone call, I scouted the room. There were only two other people in the large room. They sat together near one of the two doors along the back wall, so I moved to the corner across the room where I could see all three doors leading into the room.

I could also see one of the large computer screens where the progress of each patient was tracked as they worked their way through the surgical process. There were only two case numbers listed. One was in surgery, the other in preop. I assumed Thomas was the one in preop, but needed confirmation.

Dropping my bag on the seat of a chair, I returned to the desk as the clerk hung up the phone. "Can you tell me which number is Thomas's?" I asked, pointing to the computer screen on the wall.

The clerk consulted her computer again. "Fifty-six, twenty-six," she read from the screen.

"Thank you."

I checked the board again as I walked back to what was now my corner. His status had changed in the last few seconds from preop to in surgery.

Digging through my bag, I pulled out the big ball of multicolored yarn and the sixteen-inch knitting needle, which held half a baby hat in its center. I always had yarn and needles available to keep my hands busy when I had to wait somewhere. I settled in for what I prayed would not be a long wait. Watching the news channel on the television across the room, my fingers moved in automatic, well-practiced moves. My eyes occasionally bounced from the knitting to the television screen where some blonde talking head was grinning broadly as she reported the tragedies of the day then to the doors leading to the surgery suites.

I was halfway through a third row when a woman in navy blue scrubs and a white lab coat pushed through the door I had been watching. A police officer followed her into the room. They went to the information desk and spoke to the clerk, who nodded in my direction before returning to the book she was reading.

Laying my knitting to the side, I stood as they approached.

"Mrs. Wycoff?"

I nodded. "Yes, I'm Samantha Wycoff."

"I'm Doctor Walters. I triaged Thomas when he came into the ER," the woman said.

"How bad is he hurt?" I asked, cutting out any pleasantries she might want to indulge in.

The doctor dropped her gaze to the clipboard she carried. "He has been savagely beaten and remains unconscious. He has a broken arm, four broken ribs, along with internal bleeding and head trauma. There were also scrapes and bruises over about half of his body."

Gritting my teeth, I closed my eyes as I digested the list of damages. My anger at Velvet exploded like an atomic bomb. Taking a deep breath, I fought to contain my fury. I had to get through these next few minutes, talk to a few of Thomas's friends, before I could figure out how in the hell to get him to leave the asshole bitch he claimed to love. The animal who had put him here for the last time if I had anything to say about it.

Opening my eyes, I asked the only two questions I could think of. "Why was he rushed to surgery? Will he be all right?"

Dr. Walters grew serious as she answered the questions in reverse order. "We won't know until he regains consciousness. Only then will we be able to determine if there has been any brain damage. He was rushed to surgery because we saw on the body scan one of the broken ribs punctured his left lung remarkably close to his heart. The CAT scan also shows internal bleeding which we'll deal with as well. I'll let the OR team know you're out here waiting. They'll keep you up to date on how things are going."

I nodded and thanked the doctor before she walked away. Until that point, the police officer had remained silent. Once the doctor was gone, he stepped forward. "I'm Sergeant Benson, Miz Wycoff. I'm the one who called you."

"Yes, thank you, Sergeant. Sorry I was so abrupt on the phone."

My heart began to pound as it always did in the presence of a uniformed officer. It was not something I could explain, but men in uniforms with weapons on their hips made me extremely nervous.

He held out a large paper bag. "I took the liberty of collecting his wallet and phone from the scene. I thought you would want to hold onto them. His clothes were ripped and covered in blood and will be held as evidence of the crime. There is an inventory of those things in there as well."

I blinked back tears as I accepted the bag. "Thank you. Can you fill me in on what happened?"

"The next-door neighbor said she woke up to hear Thomas and a woman arguing. Then there were screams. By the time the neighbor dressed and stepped outside, the screams had stopped, and she saw a woman run down the street. She went back inside and called emergency services. Several other neighbors called in as well to report the disturbance."

"The woman would be his bitch of a girlfriend, Velvet Flores. She's done this before, but never this badly."

Sergeant Benson nodded. "I'll talk to Thomas in the morning once he regains consciousness. If you can talk to him, it might help as well. We'll do what we can, but even if convicted, the woman will probably just get probation, community service, and anger management classes."

"I'll see what I can do." I spoke through clenched teeth, my patience nearing its limit.

The sergeant handed me his card and took his leave. Returning to my seat, I returned to my knitting. Finishing one hat, I cast on another and kept knitting. As I did, I began to brainstorm the best way to get Velvet out of Thomas's life completely. Having friends who had been in abusive situations over the years, I knew it would not be an easy task.

I had watched crime dramas and mysteries on television for thirty-some years and was redneck enough to know the best way to keep them apart would be to plant her in the ground.

But proper revenge would take an assassin. I was a retired schoolteacher, church mouse, and a professional volunteer. I did not know anyone who might even remotely fit the description. On television and in the movies, assassins were young, gorgeous, buff men with dreamy bedroom eyes and sexy foreign accents.

For a moment, I wondered if anyone would suspect a widowed, fifty-four-year-old, church choir singing, hat knitting for charity woman of murdering her son's abusive girlfriend.

I laughed at the whimsical idea before brushing it aside as ridiculous. I could barely lift and prime the pump action shotgun tucked behind the door to my bedroom; how would I possibly take out Velvet?

§ § §

Five hats and three cups of bad vending machine coffee later, a lab coat-wearing man stepped into the room and called, "Thomas Wycoff's family?"

I stood and stepped forward, my knitting dropping from my suddenly lifeless hands. "Yes, I'm Thomas's mother."

The doctor crossed to me and stopped a yard away. He kept his back turned to the other visitors who had trickled in over the past hour. "It took longer than we originally planned because we had a hard time stopping the internal bleeding. There was more damage than initially thought, but we got everything taken care of. He is in the recovery area now," the man said without bothering to introduce himself.

I could hear an unspoken *but*. "There's something else wrong." My words were a statement, not a question.

He dropped his chin once in a nod. "He flat-lined twice during surgery, and his brain activity has slowed considerably. We won't know the extent of any brain damage until he wakes up," he answered diplomatically without pulling any punches. "A nurse will come get you in about twenty minutes, and you'll be able to go back and see him in the recovery room. In about three hours, if he remains stable, he'll be moved upstairs to the Surgical Recovery Unit."

I nodded, my heart bounding from throat to belly and back again, leaving me with a queasy feeling. "Thank you, Doctor. I'll be right here."

CHAPTER THREE

After a long, long eight days of sitting by Thomas's bed watching as machines kept him alive, I made the hardest decision of my life. Even letting Jarrod go had not been this painful. My sweet husband had set the limits and terms for end of life long before we needed to invoke them. All I had to do was sign the forms. But Thomas should have his whole life in front of him. After several discussions with his medical team, it took me another two days to accept that it was time to let my baby go.

Since Jarrod's death, Thomas and I had discussed illness and death several times. During each one, we both agreed being sustained on life support was no way to live. He had even warned me if he were to ever contract cancer or some other terminal disease, he would not seek treatment, instead choosing a swift, natural death over lingering endlessly and possibly being sicker from the so-called cures than from the disease itself.

After yet another long talk with his care team that Wednesday morning, eight days after he had been admitted, I signed the termination of care paperwork. Standing at the bedside, I took his hand and nervously rubbed the pad of my thumb over the skin between his thumb and forefinger as tears filled my eyes and overflowed to run down my cheeks.

"It's time, sweetheart. I'm sure you're probably mad I've waited this long, but I wasn't ready to let you go. The doctors say you aren't getting better so it's time. I love you, my sweet boy, and I will miss you, but you'll be happier on the other side. Say hello to your father for me."

I took a shaky breath and sniffed before I could continue. "I want to thank you for being my baby, my son, and my best friend. I want to also thank you for all you've taught me. And I promise you, I will make her pay for this."

I understood the machines were the only thing keeping his body alive, but thought I saw a relaxing of his shoulders as he prepared to pass out of this plane of existence and into the next.

Releasing his hand, I stepped back and allowed Nurse Nancy, the woman who had been Thomas's dayshift nurse during most of his stay, access to my baby. She moved systematically, switching off the life-sustaining machines one by one. In less than two minutes, only one remained lit and beeping, the one monitoring his vital signs.

My eyes remained glued to the screen as the various toned beeps for heartbeat and respiration slowed before stopping all together. Nurse Nancy turned that machine off as well.

I remained dry-eyed though my heartache nearly sent me to my knees. Taking a deep breath, I turned to the nurse as she made notes on her ever-present computer tablet. "You'll call the funeral home?"

"Yes, ma'am. We'll take care of everything. There will be some paperwork for you to sign, but it can wait until tomorrow if you don't want to wait around today. Would you like me to call anyone for you?"

"No, thank you," I answered as I slung my oversized leather purse over my shoulder. "Some of his friends are in the waiting room. They might want to come and see Thomas before—" I stopped speaking and swallowed hard.

"Don't worry, Mrs. Wycoff, I'll take care of it," Nurse Nancy assured me. "Are you sure you wouldn't like me to call someone for you?"

I shook my head as I took one last look at Thomas before walking out of the room. I did not want sympathetic friends and strangers spouting platitudes as they tried to share my grief.

My son was dead. No one could understand my feelings.

Surprisingly, what I wanted, what I needed more than my next breath, was revenge on Velvet Flores for doing this to my son.

As I waited for the elevator that would carry me down and out to the world continuing forward without Thomas, a layer of ice began to build around both my heart and my emotions. From the experience of Jarrod's death, I knew there was much to do in the next few days, and had been preparing for this day for the last four days.

It would take a handful of phone calls to set in motion the plans for his funeral and all the rituals and formalities to go with it. But the calls would wait until I returned home. I was in no condition to make them right now.

"Mama Sam?" A soft, vaguely familiar voice tinged with the typical Eastern North Carolina accent drew my attention away from an intense study of the nicks and dings on the wall above the elevator call buttons.

Turning, I barely had time to prepare before Becca Henry wrapped her arms around me and hugged me tight. "I'm so sorry," she whispered.

My body moving on autopilot, I returned her hug. "Thank you, sweetie. I'm sorry for your loss as well," I replied gently.

Becca and Thomas had been best friends since middle school. They had grown up together, cheered each other on through thick and thin, and spent innumerable weekends at one or the other's homes where they drove us parents crazy with their movie and music choices. They often introduced each other as "my sibling from another mother", which was true. I often felt I had a daughter and a son and loved them both very much.

Becca's hot tears soaked through my T-shirt. They felt as if they were burning my skin, which felt cold as dry ice in comparison. I held Becca as she sobbed. The elevator I had called for came and went. By the time she finally lifted her head and released me, my shoulder was soaked, and the elevator had come and gone several more times.

"I'm sorry," she said again as she used the soft purple bandana in her hand to pat at the wet spot on my shoulder.

"Don't worry; it's fine," I responded automatically.

"Where are you headed?" she asked, as she wiped her face, removing the makeup, and smearing her mascara and eyeliner until the black surrounding her eyes gave her the appearance of a sad, tired raccoon.

"I have to go to Thomas's place to pick up his suit and take it to the funeral home before I go home and make some calls."

"I'll go with you," Becca offered, sniffing and trying to corral her emotions.

I shook my head as the elevator dinged its arrival once again. "You don't have to do that. I'll be fine."

Once the elevator emptied of visitors and staff, I stepped onboard, not surprised when Becca ignored me and followed. We rode to the lobby in silence. Our combined sadness swirled around the metal box, tainting the air with the vinegary sourness of pain.

With each passing second and each beat of my heart, my determination to make Velvet pay grew. It was like a fast stop action film of a flower emerging from the ground, growing, and blooming all in the space of a minute. Only in my case, instead of a flower, it was my need for retribution growing, cold, sharp-edged, and diamond hard. By the time I stepped off the elevator and worked my way through the crowd waiting to board, my pain had frozen into a hatred so deep it filled every cell of my body. All the lessons I had learned in a lifetime of Sunday school classes and church services about forgiveness were lost as the need to see Velvet Flores dead consumed me.

An eye for an eye, I mused as I headed for the front door with Becca keeping pace on my left.

"How about I drive?" Becca broke the tense silence once we emerged from the too-cold hospital out onto the sidewalk.

I shrugged as I continued walking across the main driveway and into the parking lot in front of the hospital. My Jeep was straight ahead at the far side of the lot. Becca stopped once we were past the first row of cars and glanced around.

"There it is," she turned toward a bright red sportscar a dozen or so yards to our right.

"Cute car," I said, not sure how else to comment.

I had heard from Becca's mother Becca had blown her entire savings on the four-year-old car without a thought to her future. In my eyes, it was too small to be safe or practical, but I also remembered being her age and wanting what I wanted when I wanted it.

"Mom and Dad hate it, but it's fun for now. I'll be driving a minivan soon enough if Jackson has his way."

"How soon is the wedding?" I asked, remembering life would go on, even if Thomas's had ended.

"Two months and Jackson is hoping I'll come home from the honeymoon pregnant," Becca said as we climbed into the car.

My knees ground in painful protest as I bent down. I ended up falling into the low, low seat, and I had to hold my carryall on my lap. In just a few minutes, we were out of the hospital's parking lot and headed toward Thomas's neighborhood. I knotted my fingers together and tried not to wince, or grab hold of something as Becca zipped out of the parking lot, into traffic, and around other vehicles as if she were on a racetrack and not driving in downtown New Bern.

The low-sitting car was so different than riding in my SUV that I grew more and more tense. Or maybe it was the fact this would be the first time I had visited Thomas's home since he had been admitted to the hospital. I absently wondered if Velvet had bothered cleaning up since their argument, or if she was waiting for Thomas to come home and do it.

By the time Becca turned onto the road leading into Thomas's neighborhood, my nerves were beginning to shred. As she completed the sharp turn, I stared out the side window and saw a police car backed into the first driveway. I met the police officer's eyes for a microsecond before turning forward again.

Becca drove less than a block before a police siren began to sing out right behind us.

"You've got to be kidding," Becca muttered as she pulled over and parked.

I closed my eyes and dropped my head back onto the headrest and did a count of how many moving violations the girl had racked up in the eight-block drive from the hospital. Six. No seven.

The police car stopped behind us though his engine did not go silent. Twisting in my seat, I watched out the back windows between the seats as a pair of black-clad legs slowly approached the driver's side of the car.

Becca had her license, registration, and insurance information ready to hand over. Apparently, she had been through this before.

"Good morning, ladies," the officer said, folding himself in half to see through the open window at both of us.

"Good morning, Officer," Becca returned politely.

I remained silent and nodded.

"Do you know why I stopped you this morning, ma'am?" he asked without taking the paperwork from Becca's hand.

"Not really, unless you just don't like little red cars," Becca tried to lighten the mood. Her gentle joke felt flat.

"This is not a good neighborhood for you ladies to be in alone. Where are you going, and why?"

His questions seemed innocent enough, but I had a feeling there was more to his stopping us. This was also not the first time I had been stopped in this neighborhood, but I was so caught up in my own misery

I couldn't worry about what he was thinking we were going to do.

Turning my head, I stared across the car into the officer's reflective sunglasses. "We're going to my son's house. He died a few minutes ago at the hospital, and I need to collect clothes to bury him in."

I did not see any reason to sugarcoat the truth. If it would have gotten us on our way faster, I would have recited the *Gettysburg Address*, or listed all fifty states in alphabetical order. From the muscles of the man's jaw going slack, I did not think it would be necessary.

I ignored the officer's, "Oh, dear Lord, I'm so sorry for your loss," and turned to stare out the windshield again.

I closed myself down, disconnecting from the rest of the conversation to begin a mental list of everything we needed to get from Thomas's house.

A moment later, Becca started the car again and put it in gear. I watched out the side window as the houses on each block grew more desperate and broken down than the last. Finally, she stopped and turned off the engine in front of a tiny cracker box of a house with overgrown weeds for a front yard.

I climbed from the car and only then realized the police car had followed us. Becca came around the front of her car, and together, we strode up the dirt path where a sidewalk should have been.

As I studied the house, I grew more appalled that my smart, beautiful, hardworking baby boy had been reduced to living in this neglected house in a neighborhood no doubt rife with drug dealers, prostitutes, and who knows what other kind of lowlifes. Thomas's pride and determination to make it on his own without my help had brought him to this. Once he and Velvet had moved in together, I began to refuse all his requests for financial assistance because I kept hoping he would leave the bitch and move home where I would have been happy to help him get back on his feet again.

But that never happened. We were both too proud to give in.

Becca grabbed my arm as we reached the bottom of the three steps leading up to a small cement slab of a front stoop. "Something's wrong," she said softly.

"How can you tell?" I asked as my glance swept over the front of the house.

"Stay here. I'm going to get our shadow," she ignored my question.

I remained where she left me, my thoughts wandering to what I would do if we actually found Velvet inside. Would I be able to get what I needed and walk away without seeing her bleed? Or would I kill her in the name of retribution, despite the police presence?

"Excuse me, ma'am," the officer said as he eased past me and climbed the two steps to the front stoop.

Becca and I watched as he examined the door and the knob. He reached into a small pouch on his utility belt and pulled on a pair of black latex gloves. Once his hands were covered, he tested the knob and pushed the door open. At the same time, he pulled his weapon from its holster with his other hand.

"Hello? New Bern Police Department," he called before stepping through the doorway and disappeared from sight.

When I moved to follow, Becca grabbed my arm and held me back. "We'll wait right here until he says it's okay to enter."

"Yes, ma'am," I said with a smile. "You sound like you've been through this before."

"Nah, I've watched waaaaay too much crime drama on TV. I could commit the perfect crime if I weren't so legophobic."

"Legophobic?"

"Afraid to get swept into the legal system," she responded with a huffed laugh, "not a fear of Legos."

"You can come in now, ladies," the officer called from inside the house.

Becca took my hand and moved in front of me as we climbed the steps and entered the house where my son had lived for the past half year. Once inside, she squeezed my hand when I gasped at the conditions we found. Someone had trashed the house. There were clothes, food containers, beer cans, and whiskey bottles scattered across the floor. Otherwise, the place was empty. All of the furniture and Thomas's other personal possessions were gone.

I wondered for a moment if it had been Velvet moving on, or if the neighbors had broken in and helped themselves to everything before junkie squatters had moved in and trashed the place.

Looking around, I realized this was no longer the place my son had lived in for the past six months. It now appeared to be a den of something

I never wanted to think about instead of the bachelor pad I had spent two days helping him paint. The rancid smell of trash, human waste, and various smokes made me crinkle my nose in disgust as Becca began to gag.

"Why don't you wait in the yard, and I'll see if there's anything left," Becca offered even as her hand came up to cover her mouth.

I shook my head. "No, I'll go to the mall and pick up what he needs."

"I'm sorry," the officer said as he followed us out the front door. "I've got to call this in and wait for the crime scene van to arrive. But I want you ladies to get in that little car and drive straight the hell out of the neighborhood without stopping. Do you understand?"

"Yes, sir, Officer, sir," Becca snarked as she gave him a salute. She linked her left arm through my right and guided me down the path to the car. "We'll go to the mall for a suit before visiting the funeral home. Then I'll take you back to your car."

I wanted to argue I would be fine doing these painful chores alone, but could tell by Becca's expression we both knew better. So I nodded instead. "Thanks. I think that's a good plan. And if you're a good girl, I'll buy you lunch for your trouble."

"It's no trouble, Mama Sam. You know Thomas would have done the same thing if the situation were reversed."

With that, my falsely bright mood deflated like a balloon released before the knot was secured around it. After one last glance over my shoulder at the duplex, I maneuvered myself back into the passenger's seat, my vow to punish Velvet growing stronger with each beat of my heart.

CHAPTER FOUR

After we completed the errands and shared a few memories over lunch, Becca dropped me back at my car. I drove home, still feeling more than a little numb. After putting my car in the garage, I closed the garage door and walked into the kitchen. I looked around as if I had never seen the place before. I had lived here alone since Jarrod's death, but today the space felt emptier and lonelier than normal.

Always sensible, organized, and prepared, I grabbed a clean dishtowel from the drawer by the sink and a can of my favorite soda from the refrigerator. Walking into the living room I had not changed since Jarrod's death, I barely made it to the couch before everything in me collapsed.

The tears I had held back since walking from Thomas's hospital room welled up and overflowed. I held the towel to my face as I sobbed, releasing the pain that had been festering since Sergeant Benson's phone call eight days earlier.

Time lost meaning as I allowed all the pain and heartbreak, anger and hate to bubble up and out of my heart. When the tears finally stopped, I sprawled on the couch, limp, boneless, and completely drained, physically as well as emotionally.

How was I supposed to stand up, smile, and accept the hugs and condolences of all those I knew would be coming in the ensuing days? Or maybe they wouldn't and I would spend the next few days mourning Thomas alone.

How could I remain sweet and hospitable and comfort others when all I wanted was to track down Velvet Flores and make her suffer for the pain she had caused Thomas and, by extension, me?

I wanted revenge.

I needed revenge for my baby's death.

But going after that woman would have to wait until after I buried my son.

As I sat up, I noticed the layer of dust on all the furniture. Thinking back, I realized the house had not had a proper cleaning in weeks. First, the depression had held me immobile in its grip, and then I had spent the last week in the hospital with Thomas.

"Well, Mama Sam, time to clean the house so visitors won't know how truly screwed up your life really is," I told myself as I pushed up from the couch.

Two hours later, I was about halfway finished deep cleaning the part of the house where visitors would be when someone rang the doorbell.

Opening the door, I was only mildly surprised to find Becca on the other side. Multiple bulging full cloth grocery dangled from both of her hands. A moment later, Jeff and Ellen Charles, two more of Thomas's closest friends, stepped onto the porch. Jeff cradled several cases of soda to his chest while Ellen carried what I recognized as the casserole carrier I had given them as a wedding gift two years earlier.

Becca spoke for the little group. "We're here to help. What do you need us to do?"

I did not know how to answer the question. I was not sure I would be able to hand off the remaining chores that needed doing. I needed to keep myself busy so I did not have time to think too much. But these three appeared determined to be here for me and to help.

"I was cleaning," I said as Becca stepped forward, forcing me to step back out of the doorway.

Jeff followed the women to the kitchen, and returned with empty arms. "If it's all right with you, I'll cut the grass and clean up the yard."

I glanced out the front door I had yet to close. I could not remember how long it had been since I had worked in the yard, but by the overgrown appearance, I was surprised I had not heard from the homeowner's association about the grass being too tall. Maybe they had heard about Thomas and were cutting me a break, though I doubted it. The head of the association was a retired Marine and hated disorder in *his* neighborhood.

"Are you sure? You don't have to. I don't want to be a bother."

Jeff gave me a sad smile before stepping in close. He gave me a gentle bear hug as only a big man can. I blinked back more tears and hugged him. Finally, he released me and stepped away before brushing a kiss on my cheek. "I'll take care of the yard, Mama Sam. You sit down and relax. You must be exhausted after being at the hospital for the past week. Let us help you. Ellen brought dinner, and I'm sure more people will be stopping by later."

I wanted to argue with him, but nodded instead. I did not have it in me to fight him. To fight anyone.

While the cry had cleaned me out emotionally, it had also left me feeling numb. I felt like I had been wrapped in a double thick layer of bubble wrap. I remembered feeling this way in the days and weeks after Jarrod's death.

Eventually, I had begun to feel again, but ever since, I experienced everything through a filter of grief. I realized, this time, the sadness would have an added layer of anger to it.

Over the next days, Becca proved to be a godsend. She made sure I ate and drank, slept, bathed, and generally functioned as I should. She helped me deal with people who dropped by, kept track of the overwhelming amount of food people dropped off, and made a list of the offers to help from both Thomas's and my own friends and neighbors.

§ § §

During the three-hour evening visitation at the funeral home four days later, I drifted through the building like a cloud on the wind. My only conscious thought was to stay as far from the room where Thomas's casket sat as I could without being too obvious about it. I let Becca, Jeff, and the others hold court in the room where my son lay in repose while I circled the other rooms, accepting condolences and comforting others. I heard, but did not respond to the whispered comments of pity, gossip, and speculation as I wandered the building. I shook hands, accepted hugs, and greeted people with a few words and a sad smile before moving on to the next group.

Toward the end of the evening, I needed a break from the feeling of having a microscope focused on my every move, so I escaped to the ladies' room. The cloyingly sweet, flower-scented air freshener they used tickled my nose, but I ignored it and took a deep cleansing breath. I held it for a count of twenty before releasing it on a long sigh. I was alone, at least for a few minutes. I had no doubt Becca would send someone to check on me if I did not reappear in the next five minutes, but that was okay. For now, there was no one watching me, judging me, making me feel as if I were responsible for Thomas's death instead of the real culprit, Velvet Flores.

Stopping in the middle of the well-appointed restroom with its padded Pepto-Bismol pink chaise lounge in one corner and boxes of tissues on every flat surface in sight, I wrapped my arms around my middle. Closing my eyes, I forced myself to stand still and focus on breathing.

In. Out. In. Out. In. Out.

I kept it up until the need to screech like an alley cat with its tail on fire eased. I had always hated gossips, and now being the focus of their attention made me crazy. I forced myself to take in two more slow, deep breaths. Somehow, some way, I would get through the next twenty-four hours. I would bury Thomas next to Jarrod and survive the post burial reception.

Then, after a day or two, I would work to regain my footing on the new life path of aloneness I would be traveling from here on out. If I could find Velvet and make her pay for what she had taken from me then maybe, just maybe the growing thirst for revenge which had taken residence between my heart and stomach might be slaked.

I hoped.

My time alone and undisturbed was about up, so I took one last deep breath and held it for as long as I could before slowly releasing it again. With my emotional armor back in place I could return to the gathering. Checking my watch, I hoped the crowd was beginning to thin out.

When I stepped out of the restroom into the hall, I was not surprised to find one of Thomas's friends standing right outside. The identity of the person leaning against the wall like he would be willing to wait all day if he had to did surprise me.

"Micah Kendrick," I murmured as the tall, powerfully built man with his jet-black hair cut military short straightened.

He had grown taller, broader, and more muscled since I'd last seen him. The Marines had done a good job training him as he stood straight and tall, looking like a hurricane would not knock him off his feet.

"Mama Sam," he said as tears filled his pale silver-blue eyes.

He crossed the hall in two strides and wrapped long, thickly muscled arms around me in a warm embrace. I could do nothing but wrap my arms around his waist and hug him back. It felt like I was hugging a warm rock and not a man; he was that toned.

Micah Kerrick was the closest thing Thomas had had to an older brother. He was three years older than Thomas's twenty-four years, and had lived next door with his parents until he graduated from high school and left home to join the Marines.

In the years since, Micah had faithfully sent me cards each year at Christmas and on my birthday. Each one contained a short note, vaguely describing what he'd been doing and that he hoped to see me soon. While in the service, he never let on where he was. The FPO postmarks told me most of the cards came from out of the country. The past few years, the cards had all come from the same Silver Springs, Maryland, postmark though he never put a return address on them, so I could never respond with a card of my own or care package of homemade goodies.

"It's so good to see you," I whispered as I tried to pull back from the embrace.

He released me, but grabbed my arm and pinched me hard on the back of my left upper arm. He squeezed the flesh tight between his finger and thumb even as I tried to pull my arm away.

"Ouch! What was that for?" I yelled even as the emotional bubble wrap surrounding my emotions popped and ripped away. The red-hot pain and anger I had packed away swept through me like floodwaters breeching a dam.

"You seemed like you're about to explode and need the release," he answered simply as he released the skin and grabbed more an inch further down my upper arm.

Stepping close to him again, I rested my forehead on the front of his shoulder. The tears I had hoped to keep at bay until tomorrow after the funeral welled up, broke out, and overflowed. When I began to tremble, his arms tightened around my back, and I ended up leaning heavily against him. His gentle, yet strong-armed hug shredded the last of the barrier, and I broke down completely.

My brain shut out everything and everyone except the pain, which had continued to fester in my heart and soul. I did not hear the conversations around me. I did not hear plans being made for my immediate future. When Micah began to move, I went with him, my arms holding tight to his waist like an octopus's tentacles hugging a rock. I was not letting go of this man any time soon. But since his arms remained tight around my back and shoulders as well, it appeared I didn't have to worry about losing his support.

When I finally cried myself out and was able to lift my head from his chest, I found we had moved to the parking lot behind the funeral home. Micah was leaning against one of those ginormous black SUVs with windows tinted so dark it could only belong to a rap star, a drug dealer, or a government agent.

For the first time in days, there was no one else around watching me. No one fussing at me, asking questions, making demands, or offering opinions. Even the sounds of New Bern after dark were muted, with only an occasional car driving down Neuse Boulevard in front of the funeral home to disturb the quiet.

"Take some time to relax, and just breathe," he said softly.

One big hand began to move up and down my spine in long, soothing strokes. The touch helped relax something deep inside me, something that had been tied in knots since Jarrod's death.

It took a few minutes before I felt stable enough, and strong enough, to back away. Taking a deep shuddering breath, I pulled an oversized bandana out of my jacket pocket and mopped up.

Once I had myself under an illusion of control, I began to pace in a circle. I moved between the SUV he leaned against and Becca's little red sports car two spaces over.

"Feel better?"

I shrugged as I wrapped my arms around my middle. I could not tell if the chill I felt came from the night air, which continued to cool quickly, or if I was just trying to hold myself together. Shivers raced through me at irregular intervals.

"I know you might not want to talk about it yet, but can you tell me what happened to Thomas?" he asked, his deep voice heavily laced with compassion.

I felt like my stomach turned itself inside out as I slowly shifted to face him. Stepping back, I leaned against Becca's car and moved my head left to right and back again several times.

"Let's just say Thomas's taste in women has not improved since he brought home Millie Vann in seventh grade."

Micah frowned as he thought back. "Wasn't she the one who took him out back of your shed to smoke, only he threw up all over her, and they caught the shed on fire?"

I smiled sadly at the memory. "Yeah, that's the one. Only this one beat Thomas. This wasn't the first time she'd hurt him, but this time it was so bad he ended up brain dead."

"Damn," Micah shifted his feet farther apart before sliding his hands into the pockets of his black tactical pants. His expression grew cold and hard. His voice, when he spoke, took on an Italian gangster accent. "You want I should disappear her? I can do it. I know people who would happily hunt her down for a twelve-pack of beer. They even have a woodchipper and a four-wheel drive truck to finish the job. Her body would never be found."

He looked deadly serious, and I could not suppress a smile at his hokey accent. He had always loved mafia movies when he was younger and apparently remained a fan to this day.

His offer caused my need for revenge to roar back to life like fresh kindling tossed onto white-hot coals. "No, I don't want you to make her disappear. I want to do it myself ... but I may need your help."

Chapter Five

The Present

A soft double-tap of knuckles on the bathroom door jolted me back into the present. It was time to go to work. Every muscle in my body tightened with nerves and stress as I unlocked the door and eased it open. I was half expecting another guest to be on the other side, waiting to use the bathroom. My breath whooshed out when I found Micah standing on the other side appearing nearly as tense as I felt.

"Ready?"

At my quick nod, he turned and started down the hall. Grabbing the rifle, I hurried to follow him. I held the weapon low, keeping it hidden in my skirt with the muzzle pointed toward the floor.

I'd been taught gun safety on my second date with Jarrod when he took me to a shooting range for an afternoon of what he liked to call bang-bang therapy. I was surprised when I did indeed feel more relaxed after a day of blowing holes in paper targets as I learned to shoot.

Jarrod's rules were simple and stayed with me even to this day. Never point a weapon at anyone or anything unless you are prepared to shoot it. Always keep your weapon clean and ready to fire. Never ever, ever, ever, ever assume any weapon is unloaded unless you have confirmed it yourself.

As we hurried silently and cautiously down the hall, I kept glancing behind me, watching for anyone who might come up the staircase behind us or pop out of one of the closed doors that lined the hall. It felt like it took forever to reach the door at the end of the hall.

We finally made it, and Micah eased the door open. After sticking his head in and looking around to make sure the room was empty, he once again proved he was a gentleman and stepped back to allow me to scurry past him. He followed me inside and pushed the door closed behind him. I relaxed only minimally after hearing the soft snick of the lock being engaged.

Micah touched my shoulder to get my attention and pointed toward the window to the right of the king-size bed across the room. It was one of four windows in the room, none of which had curtains covering them. From the stale feel to the air, and the open suitcase lying open on the wooden chest at the foot of the bed, this was a guestroom, one not often used.

I pushed down every thought but those concerning the next few minutes and moved toward the window. My brain ticked through the sequence of events to be executed in the next ten minutes. We had rehearsed this scenario dozens of times over the last five days, and I knew each move to make from now until Brooklyn Brown picked me up out front once I left the party. We even covered every glitch Micah's team could come up with, working them into various trial runs so I would not freak out if something went sideways, which, according to Brooklyn, always happened.

My heart pounded like a bass drum in a patriotic march as I worked to keep my breathing slow and steady. Holding the gun in my left hand, I clenched and unclenched my right hand while flexing the wrist in preparation.

Micah unlocked and manhandled the bottom panel of the window, lifting it only far enough for me to slide the gun barrel and scope through the opening. Pulling my skirt up with my free hand, I knelt in front of the window.

"How are you feeling?" Micah whispered as he knelt beside me with his handy-dandy spotter's monocle at the ready.

I nodded instead of speaking, not wanting to think about anything but what I needed to do next. While I had been nervous, almost petrified, as I waited for things to begin, now we were actually doing something and working through the list of actions previously drilled into me. My emotions shifted. I thought of Thomas, and the familiar anger toward the woman who had killed him counteracted the fear. I shut my emotions down until I felt emotionally numb and ice cold.

The icy chill I felt emanated from the inside out. The late December breeze coming through the open window might have had something to with it, but I didn't think so. It was imperative the next few minutes were a success. This was my test. Pass it and I would become a member of Micah's Misfits. Fail and I was not sure what would happen, but from veiled comments from the rest of the team, I would either end up dead or turned in to the police to take the fall for a murder, even if it weren't the one I was currently involved in committing.

I'm doing this for Thomas, I reminded myself as I took my position. I studied the balconies on the building across the street through the scope's site.

My target was a so-called foreign diplomat who liked to break laws, not only of his own country, but also the United States and every other country in the world. Drugs, guns, trafficking young girls and boys, this guy used his position in his country's government to deal in anything shady to line his pockets.

The report Micah had shown me revealed he liked to spend his evenings at his personal assistant's apartment, drinking the finest vodka before having violent sex with the woman. Once he finished with her for the evening, he would go home to his society wife who had her own string of lovers. He preferred to have sex on the balcony of the assistant's apartment late at night because he liked to hear her screams echo up and down the street. He was also known to bring young girls to the woman's apartment and use them as well, giggling with glee as the girls' high pitched screams filled the near silence of Old Town late at night.

The more I had been told about this animal with diplomatic immunity, the more my stomach turned. He was a sick, twisted son of a bitch who needed to be put out of the world's misery. Just like Velvet Flores. And a couple dozen other assholes I could list off the top of my head who thought they were above the law. Maybe I should stop watching the news and take offense at the insanity the judicial system seemed to indulge in of late.

Since starting to work with Micah, I had begun a list. I added names to it almost weekly as news stories broke online and on television about rapists, murderers, and other criminals who either got away with their crimes due to rich white privilege, victim intimidation, or twisting the truth so their victims were blamed for living their lives instead of the criminals being blamed for indulging their dark sides. I had begun a second list of names of the police officers, judges, and others in the legal system who had ignored the law and allowed these criminals to go free.

People like Velvet.

I was not one of those strait-laced, tight-assed, Southern women who only made love in the missionary position under the covers with the lights out. But to me, sex on a balcony in the middle of December where anyone passing by might glance up and watch was batshit crazy.

But we were not here to kill the man outright. He would not die tonight. Putting a bullet in his head to kill him outright would start a war, or some equally devastating international incident. And that's not what Micah and his team did. We were here because someone in a government office somewhere had decided this monster with diplomatic immunity from U.S. prosecution needed "to be dealt with," as Micah had so eloquently termed it.

But he could not die on American soil. He could not die of a gunshot wound. It had to appear like he died of natural causes or some sort of accident. And that was where Micah, his team, and I came into play. It was our job to set the man up for dying off United States soil.

"Second balcony from this end of the building on the third floor." Micah's whispered words tickled my ear.

I shifted slightly, staring down the side of the gun to spot the balcony before shifting my gaze to the rifle's scope to sight in. As I did, my heart began to pound even harder. I watched through the wall of windows beyond the balcony as our target ripped the clothes from the woman's body before stripping himself. I fought not to gag at the sight of his bloated, overweight, pasty white body.

Seconds later, the sliding glass door to the balcony slid open. Our target, Nicoli something or other, whose last name I could not pronounce, stepped outside. He pulled the resistant woman along behind him with his fleshy hand wrapped around her neck.

They were both naked, which caused me to shiver in sympathy for the woman. Taking a slow, deep breath, I forced all thoughts away except what I was to do next. Releasing the breath, I emotionally stepped back, becoming an observer of the scene, an emotionless robot watching in preparation for the job at hand.

The woman was a tight-bodied natural blonde whose carpet matched the drapes, and apparently a regular patron at both a gym and a tanning salon. With all the maintenance she needed, how did she have time to have a job? Or maybe the job was a ruse as well as everything else about Nicoli whatever's life appeared to be.

Nicoli, no, *the target*, I reminded myself sternly, looked like he had never set foot inside a gym and had skin so pale it glowed in the small amount of light from the street. I also noted he had no body hair, other than the greased 1950s styled black hair on the top of his head and the full, bushy beard and mustache that, in my opinion, needed a trim.

He pulled the woman across the balcony. She was talking, pleading, no doubt trying to convince him to go back inside. He slapped her face, sending her stumbling toward the balcony wall. She stopped fighting when he wrapped his arms around her, and pulled her in for a bearhug.

Disgusted by the display, I forced myself to continue watching through the scope. In the next moment, they began to kiss, exchanging sloppy open-mouthed kisses, which made my stomach turn further. Or was it the nasty crabby mushroom I'd eaten downstairs, making itself known again?

Finally, Nicoli broke the kiss and released the woman. She took one step toward the door before he slammed his hands down on her shoulders. I could not see her face, but felt sympathy for her as he forced her down and out of sight behind the metal panel that made up the balcony's railing. He shifted so his back was to the street. My nose wrinkled as I realized he was demanding a blowjob.

Beside me, Micah huffed his amusement.

"Get ready," he breathed. His words sounded too loud in the silent room.

I fought the urge to take my eye from the scope and look around to confirm we were still alone in the room. Instead, I took another breath, adjusting the scope to zero in on the thick, meaty flesh of asshole diplomat's upper back. This was not to be a kill shot through the heart, lungs, or brain. This would simply be a delivery shot, and the fleshy part of his back over his shoulder would work perfectly for what the contents of the bullets would deliver.

The darts I had loaded in the rifle contained a tranquilizer as well as a liquid filled with nanobots and a designer virus, which would lie dormant in his body until he left the country and passed through TSA scanners. It did not matter if he left the country in a few hours as expected, or a few days, or even next year.

The quick acting tranquilizer would take less than twenty seconds to kick in and would knock the man out just long enough for the assistant to pluck the dart from his back and toss it over the railing. Once he woke up, he would be on his way back to his wife, and two agents from

WitSec would sweep in and relocate his assistant to Kansas City to start her new life.

Apparently everyone could be bought, for the right price.

The nanobots in the dart were programmed not to go active until he passed through the full body scanner at the airport—the same scanner everyone who flew had to pass through. It did not matter their age, race, or diplomatic status, whether they were flying commercial or private, everyone who flew out of Reagan National or Dulles Airports had to pass through the scanner, which would activate the virus and microscopic bots.

Once the trigger was pulled, the clock would begin running, and seventy-five hours after passing through the scanner, Nicoli would drop dead of an apparent heart attack. At his age, and with his weight, and physical conditions, no one would think it was anything else. And no one would suspect the crasher of a holiday party he had not attended to be responsible for his murder.

"Anytime now, Mama," Micah encouraged softly.

I ignored him, watching as the woman used whatever skills she had, to wind the man up tighter and tighter. Another few seconds and I could see by his profile he was close to his orgasm. Very, very close.

As thoroughly instructed over the past months, I quickly went through my shooting protocol that ended with me pulling the trigger. The rifle made a soft sound and twitched slightly in my hands. I saw a dart penetrate his body just under his shoulder blade at the same time he arched his back, threw his head back and roared out his orgasm.

He did not even realize he had been shot.

As soon as I fired the second shot, hitting an inch below the first, Micah pulled the gun out of my hands. I wanted to watch the rest of the drama play out, but knew we had to go.

Micah sent out a two-word message to Brooklyn and the WitSec team: *Mission accomplished.*

"Good job," he said with an almost smile on his lips. "Time to go, before someone misses us downstairs."

"You're paying for a decent meal after this, right?" I stated as my stomach gave a rumble, reminding me the only thing I had eaten since lunch had been that damned mushroom.

"Absolutely," he grinned and winked at me. "And if you're a good girl and don't get stopped on the way out, you can even have dessert."

I released the weapon to his more than capable hands before using the windowsill to regain my footing and stand. Once on my feet, I wiped my still gloved hand over the windowsill to make sure nothing had been left behind. Lifting my skirt, I retrieved the cloth pouch from the garter wrapped around my thigh. Micah quickly disassembled the weapon and had the scope and firing mechanism ready to drop in the bag by the time I unzipped it.

He took the pouch and tucked it somewhere out of sight. Brushing a kiss on my cheek, he smiled at me through the dark and whispered, "You were amazing, Mama Sam. Now get your ass downstairs and make your excuses. I'll see you in the car."

Adrenaline pumped through me so hard I developed a sudden headache so I would not have to feign one, which would have been my excuse to leave the party early. At the hall door, I stopped and took several deep breaths, hoping to slow my heart rate and ease the pain in my temples. The last thing I needed was someone to notice I was not the calm, cool, completely forgettable lady no one at the party knew I had been ten minutes ago.

Micah clearing his throat behind me got me moving again. I unlocked the hall door and pulled it open far enough to slip through. I glanced back at Micah, and he gave me an encouraging nod just before I pulled the door closed. While I headed downstairs to the party, he would stop in another room down the hall and toss the ceramic gun out a window. It was supposed to hit the street below and shatter into a zillion pieces of sand and never be identified as a weapon outlawed by the government over forty years earlier.

As I racewalked down the hall to the stairs, I took a second to wonder how Micah would get away from the catering crew he had come in with. Then I mentally shook myself. I did not need to be worrying about him right now. I needed to remain focused on getting myself out the front door and into the rented limousine without too many questions being asked.

Slowing my pace down the stairs, I paused on the bottom step for several seconds. Taking one last steadying breath, I stepped to the cloakroom and gave the girl the ticket for my cloak. I also asked her to call for my car to be brought around.

I entered the living room and made one last rapid circuit before finding the host and hostess. I explained the growing migraine and included happy birthday and happy holiday wishes with my good-bye. Receiving sympathetic noises and advice from the hostess, I made my way back to the cloakroom as dinner was announced and everyone else headed for the dining room.

The girl handed over my cloak and said my car should be waiting out front.

Less than ten minutes after firing the two biobullets, which began the countdown on Nicoli's life, I slipped my arms into the luxurious floor-length black velvet cloak with the red satin lining that had been delivered to my hotel room shortly after I arrived earlier in the afternoon. I did not have a hard time keeping a pained expression on my face because my temples pounded from the still fast flowing adrenaline, which kept my blood pressure elevated. With all I had done earlier and now to have the honest-to-God liveried butler open the front door for me, I felt very much like Jessica Bond, girl spy.

I bit the inside of my cheek as I made my way out the front door. Now was absolutely the worst moment to dissolve into hysterical giggles.

I thanked the butler as I stepped through the door and started down the half dozen brick steps leading to the sidewalk.

I moved slow and silent, trying not to grin at the three male valets whose attention remained riveted on the balcony across and half a block down the street. Nicoli, the asshole diplomat, had the secretary bent over the balcony railing, as he noisily moaned and grunted behind her. Her breasts were on full bouncing display as her lower chest rested on the railing and her arms flailed around as she tried to find something to hold onto.

I frowned. Why hadn't the tranquilizer kicked in yet? Had the darts not worked?

"Oh, excuse us, ma'am," one apologized as the black Lincoln Town Car I had arrived and pulled to a stop at the curb.

The second man offered his hand to assist me down the last few wet steps onto the sidewalk as my driver climbed out and rounded the front of the car. I slowly crossed the sidewalk, arriving at the curb as Brooklyn Brown opened the back door.

The valet beside me gaped at the man. While I would not be

remembered, my dark-skinned, six-and-a-half-foot tall, three hundred pounds of thickly muscled driver might. Especially since his normal expression was pissed-off and ready to kill a rock. Brooklyn was not only my driver, but also acting as my bodyguard in Micah's absence.

When his eyes met mine, I dropped my head an inch and allowed a slight grin of victory to emerge. He blinked before allowing himself a slight nod in return as he opened the back door. Giving the valet a glare, the man backed away quickly, and Brooklyn helped me into the back seat.

He closed the door and rounded the back of the car before taking his place in the driver's seat. Seconds later, the car smoothly pulled away from the curb. We were two blocks from the scene of my first government-sanctioned assassination when it hit me:

I had just killed a man.

Oh, sure, he was not dead yet, but eventually he would leave the country and die, and it would be my fault. Even though he more than deserved to die for his many, many unpunished crimes against the human race, he had never done anything to me personally. He was not the one responsible for my son's death. He was the means to an end.

This evening had allowed me to get revenge on Velvet Flores.

All at once, my stomach turned over. The mushroom cap and ginger ale I had consumed at the party were about to make a repeat appearance.

"Brooklyn," I cried, covering my mouth with one hand as I leaned forward and reached out to him with the other. He would be prepared for this. He was prepared for any contingency.

Without a word, or even a glance in my direction, the big, bald, Black man reached to the seat beside him. He picked something up and flicked his wrist before extending his arm over the seat toward me. He held an airsick bag.

I had just enough time to jerk the open end of the bag to my face before I threw up everything I had eaten since arriving in town the day before, or at least that was what it felt like.

Once I finished being sick, I carefully folded the top over and secured it, placed it into the gallon-size zippered bag Brooklyn handed me next. After flattening the bag and securing the zippered closure, I placed it back onto Brooklyn's plate-sized palm. He made it disappear while I opened the car's bar compartment and pulled out a bottle of water.

I rolled down the window and took a swig of water, then leaned out of the window and spat, hoping I did not hit the car. Another swish and spit helped wash the sour taste of stomach acid from my mouth. By the time I rolled up the window and collapsed back against the seat, the adrenaline rush I had been riding washed through my body and out my toes, leaving me drained and hungry.

Closing my eyes against the pain continuing to pound in my head, I once again asked myself, "How the hell did I get here?"

CHAPTER SIX

The Past

I woke the morning of Thomas's funeral in my own bed and fully clothed, except for my shoes, lying on top of the comforter with my favorite fleece blanket over me. A bottle of water and two extra strength, over-the-counter painkillers waited on my bedside table.

I lay still, staring at the ceiling, trying to remember how I had gotten here. Micah, Becca, and a few of Thomas's closest friends had followed me home after the visitation. Someone had brought several bottles of alcohol, which we proceeded to consume. I drank steadily from the seemingly bottomless shot glass as his friends shared stories and memories until the wee hours of the morning.

My last memory was of staring into the empty red plastic shot glass and trying to remember if that was my fourth or fifth shot of whatever strong alcoholic brew was being mixed. For someone who did not normally drink, I thought I had kept up well with the younger generation.

At least for a while.

It had been fun listening to and laughing at their stories and memories of Thomas and the antics he had pulled during his teenage years, most of which I had never heard about. I wished I could remember how I had gotten into my bed and who I would find when I dared to leave my room.

Shifting around on the bed, I moved my arms and legs, then slowly rolled over, and pushed myself up so I was sitting with my legs hanging over the side of the bed. I groaned as a hammer began to drive nails into my skull, proving once again there was a reason I didn't drink more than one alcoholic beverage at any event where alcohol was served.

Reaching toward the nightstand, I quickly popped the painkillers in my mouth and washed them down with half the bottle of water. After emitting a not-so-ladylike burp, I slowly pushed myself off the bed and tried not to stagger as I headed to the bathroom.

It was time to get the second worst day of my life started.

During the long, hot shower, I thanked God for the tankless water heater, which allowed me to stand under the nearly scalding spray until I felt somewhat human. After climbing out and drying off, I did my hair before dressing in the same basic black T-shirt dress I had worn for Jarrod's funeral. It had hung in the back of my closet since his funeral, and I had already decided that, after washing it tomorrow, I would donate it somewhere.

I would never wear it again.

Opening my bedroom door, I didn't see bodies lying all over the living room, which was a good thing. As I made my way to the kitchen, I found Micah asleep on the couch in the living room, wrapped in the quilt I kept tucked away on the bottom shelf of the bookcase along the wall. He seemed different than he had the night before. Less hardened Marine veteran and more relaxed.

I tried to be quiet as I entered the kitchen to start the day. The first task of every morning was to start the coffee. Once the coffeemaker went to work, I pulled one of the many breakfast casseroles people had dropped off out of the refrigerator and put it in the oven, which I turned on.

The aroma of fresh brewed coffee had begun to scent the air when Micah appeared in the kitchen doorway. His feet were bare, but he still wore the black polo and cargo pants from the night before. With a grunted "Morning," he poured himself a cup of coffee and walked out of the kitchen again.

Unable to help myself, I drifted to the kitchen doorway in order to watch him walk out the front door, and wondered about his plans. He left the door standing open and returned two minutes later, carrying a suitcase in one hand and a hanging bag draped over his shoulder. He sipped at his coffee as he used his hip to bump the door closed.

Without a glance in my direction, he disappeared down the hallway where the guest rooms were located. A few minutes later, I heard the shower go on in the hall bathroom. I listened until the water stopped and silence descended over the house once more.

Except for Thomas staying over an occasional night or two, there had not been a man in the house since Jarrod's passing. It felt strange to have someone else in the house.

Micah entered the kitchen twenty minutes later, wearing perfectly tailored black dress pants, a white shirt, and shiny black shoes. He carried a black dress coat in one hand that he laid over the end of the couch. A glimpse of his tie and I grinned at the same time my eyes filled with tears. It was a black tie with a black and white picture of Winnie the Pooh and his friends on it. I blinked rapidly as I recalled giving him that tie as a high school graduation present, just days before he left for the Marines. It had been a joke between us to remind him not to take life too seriously.

"I can't believe you kept that tie," I said as I pulled the casserole from the oven and carried it to the kitchen table. I had not bothered setting the table, just laid out real silverware. Becca had set up a spot on the table with a tall stack of paper plates and plastic forks and spoons in plastic cups so I would not have to worry about doing dishes.

Micah smoothed one hand over his tie as he grinned at me. "One of my favorite ladies gave this to me. I thought she would appreciate me wearing it today."

My mouth went dry as I thought of the Marine hardened body hidden by the shirt and tie. Embarrassed by the feelings the sight of the young man's flat belly brought up in me, I turned away. As I did, I reminded myself I was old enough to be his mother.

I had no interest in men half my age. Or men my age. Or any age. I'd had my one true love and did not see myself loving another man in this lifetime. With a deep breath, I retrieved the coffeepot and refilled his empty mug and my own.

Once we settled on opposite sides of the table with the warmed casserole between us, I focused on breakfast. As I ate, I began to compile a mental list of everything I needed to do to get it through the rest of the day. My meltdown in Micah's arms and drinking the night before had relieved some the emotional pressure that had built up in me like a too-full helium balloon.

I was once again able to think and plan somewhat clearly. With luck, I would make it through the funeral and reception afterward without any further emotional outbursts. I needed to be strong for everyone around me, just like I'd been for Jarrod's funeral.

Once I was alone again, I would let go and cry myself an ocean of tears.

§ § §

During the funeral, I sat stoically in the front row of the church with Micah on my right and Becca on my left. Becca's parents sat on the other side of her. I had only been mildly surprised after breakfast when I played the messages on the machine and my brother and sister had left messages saying they would not be attending the service. Both messages had been left the night before while I was at the visitation.

Their messages were nearly identical with regrets at being unable to attend, but neither gave any further explanation. Those calls solidified my feelings of being completely alone in the world.

As Thomas had told me at Jarrod's visitation when they had again been noticeably absent, "Mom, they're blood, but we're family."

As a group of Thomas's church friends sang an appropriate hymn Becca had helped me choose, I wondered how long it would be until I was once again back at Union Point, staring across the wide black river, contemplating the long swim toward my own funeral.

I kept my head up and back straight. The last thing I needed was for someone in the church to guess at my dark, dark emotions. The only one who had seen the soul deep, intense anger simmering deep inside me was Micah. He now sat close enough the shoulder and upper arm of his black suit coat pressed against my arm. His simple touch kept me grounded and on an emotionally even keel as the service lumbered on for what seemed like forever. Thomas would have hated the fuss.

When the minister stood to give his homily on Thomas's too short life, my thoughts wandered to how to track Velvet Flores down, and put her in a box without getting caught. Her coffin would bear no resemblance to the beautiful walnut casket Thomas now rested in which was the identical match for the one we had chosen for his father. She would be in a cardboard box in a pauper's grave, or better yet, a rusty coffee can after being cremated, or just left out for the gators in a swamp somewhere outside of town without a headstone or a church service to mark her passing. I did not care which, as long as she ended up as dead as my beautiful son.

That was if her body was even found. Having been hunting and hiking in eastern North Carolina with Jarrod for the last thirty years, I knew of more than a few swampy areas where gators and bears and other critters lived. Places where a body would never ever be found.

I came back to the present with a jolt when Micah laid a hand on my knee. The service was over. He helped me stand then stayed close, often with one arm around my back as all those who had attended the service filed by. They shook my hand or leaned in and gave me a quick hug, once again murmuring words of condolence and empty offers of assistance that meant little to me and barely registered.

I forced myself to smile and nod, thankful the graveside portion of the service had been canceled due to a rainstorm, which had begun as people were arriving for the service. All I had to do was get through the post-funeral reception in the fellowship hall across the way from the sanctuary. As soon as it ended, I could go home and grieve.

Once I got past the worst of my grief, I would begin making plans to gain my revenge.

Micah placed my hand on his elbow, covering it with his own to hold it in place, refusing to let me pull away as we followed the last of the mourners from the sanctuary, out of the church building, through the drizzle to the reception hall across the courtyard. We left the team from the funeral home to deal with getting the casket to the cemetery and buried appropriately. That was when I realized for the first time I would not be alone to face the crowd. Micah had apparently taken on the assignment to escort, guard, protect, shadow.

I loved Becca, but in her current do-do-do mindset, she was too exhausting for my current mental state. Micah was a calmer, steadier personality to deal with, though he had yet to respond to my request for his assistance in gaining revenge on Thomas's killer.

Two hours later, the last of the mourners finally drifted out of the hall and returned to their own lives. When I tried to help with the cleanup, the church volunteers shooed me out of the kitchen and told me to go home and relax. Micah escorted me to his SUV without a word. He kept the conversation light as he drove us back to my house and parked in the driveway.

I walked through the front door to a sparkling clean house. Someone had come by while we were gone and thoroughly cleaned the house. Becca had no doubt sent them. The silence in the house felt like a cheese grater running across my nerves. Without glancing at Micah, who had silently followed me into the house, I stepped into the living room, reached for the remote, and turned on the television.

When the canned laughter of an inane teenage comedy filled the silence, I winced. I flipped through a dozen channels before turning the television off again.

"What are you going to do now, Samantha?"

I realized he had stopped calling me Mama Sam as he and all of Thomas's other friends had done for most of my son's life. Since my meltdown in the parking lot the night before, he had used my full name, something not even my closest friends did. I had been Sam or Mama Sam for far too many years to think about. But now, to him at least, I was Samantha.

I just wished I knew who Samantha Wycoff was these days.

Not sure exactly why he had asked, it felt like the question might be leading to something important. I took the easy way out. "Well, after I change into something a little more comfortable, I'm going to wash this dress and put it in the donation box I keep in the garage. Though I've only worn it a total of three times, I will never ever wear it again. Then I guess I'll figure out which of the dozen casseroles in the fridge we're going to eat for dinner. Or will you be heading home now the pomp and ceremony are done?"

Micah crossed the room to stand in front of me. He laid his big, warm hands on my shoulders to keep me from moving away. "That's not what I meant, and you know it. What are you going to do with the rest of your life? You are too young, too alive, to close yourself up in this house and wait to die."

Out of nowhere, rage unlike anything I had ever felt before boiled up in me. Planting my hands on his chest, I shoved hard. He took a single step back as he met my glare without a hint of fear in his calm, relaxed expression.

"I am hardly a young woman anymore. What am I supposed to do? My husband is dead. My son is dead. I'm retired and would not go back into teaching even if I could. I have no new career goals, no purpose, no reason to keep living other than to seek revenge on the woman who beat Thomas to the point he could not recover. And since murder is about as illegal as it gets, I don't see that happening anytime soon. Like Becca, I'm a legophobic, even if I am probably the last person anyone would suspect of killing another human being."

Micah began to smile as he stepped forward and returned his hands to my shoulders. Strong fingers began to massage the muscles across the tops of my shoulders pulled so tight with stress they burned with pain. Then he leaned in until we were eye-to-eye. "And that's exactly why you're going to come work with me."

As his fingertips continued to press deep into the knotted-up muscles of my shoulders, I had to lock my knees to keep from melting into a puddle from the stress relief that came from the massage. The muscles untied themselves with a different sort of pain. I had not realized how tense I was until the tension suddenly drained away.

"Work with you? How can I work with you? I don't even know what you do these days. And I'm fairly certain I don't possess a lot of the vital and necessary skills required for whatever super-secret government job it is you do now."

"Would you be willing to learn a few skills? Skills that could lead to a career that would take you all over the country and maybe the world? Skills that will, eventually, allow you to get your revenge in Thomas's name, though it may not be quite the way you're picturing right now?"

His questions, along with the strange glint in his eye, made me hesitate. After a moment, I began to nod slowly. I had always loved learning new things. After Jarrod's death, I had thought about going back to school to take some random continuing education courses, but the community college had closed down their continuing education program. Instead, they focused on offering courses strictly related to job training, not learning simply for the love of it. Even with a third to half my life ahead of me, it seemed a little late to start a new career, but I had to admit I was curious about what Micah was offering.

"I am what my employers politely call a troubleshooter. I lead a team of three other people. We clean up messes and untangle complicated situations in expeditious and definitive manners. You'll need to be vetted and approved by my boss, and his bosses, but I think you'd be the perfect addition to my team. As you said, in nearly any room, in any crowd, a widowed, over fifty, retired schoolteacher would be the least likely suspect to any nefarious deed."

His explanation left me even more confused than before. "Are you deliberately being vague to confuse me, or have I lost my ability to translate manspeak?"

Instead of answering my questions, Micah chuckled as he squeezed my shoulders before releasing me and taking a step back. "Go change into walking clothes and sneakers," he directed.

I blinked at the sudden change in the conversation. "Why?"

"Because we're going to start your training," he stated before turning and heading toward the guest wing.

"My training?"

Micah paused in the hall outside Thomas's old room. The room he had taken as his own. He grinned at me like a kid about to be let loose in a candy store with a twenty dollar bill.

"Yes, your training. You've got to start training if you're going to run the 5K on New Year's Day. I know you've always wanted to run that race and we can use it as your final test before becoming a full-fledged member of my team."

I wondered what the other tests would be, but at the moment was too afraid to ask. Instead, I went and put on my sneakers.

CHAPTER SEVEN

I stared through the scope of Jarrod's favorite hunting rifle, trying to pick out Velvet in the crowd dancing and milling about in the front yard of what had been Thomas's duplex. I could not decide which black-haired woman wearing tighter-than-skin clothes and sky-high hooker heels was the woman I was gunning for.

I had met Velvet Flores twice, which was two times too many for my taste. She was a beautiful Hispanic woman with long black hair, wearing a pound of makeup, which made her skin appear flawless. I now wished I had paid more attention to her, taken a selfie with the two of them, or something. Anything to help me pick her out of this crowd.

I had been working nonstop to find her in the three weeks since Thomas's funeral and this was the closest I had come.

My first stop the day after the funeral was to meet and talk with Marta, the woman who lived in the other half of the duplex. She was the one who had called the police the night Thomas was beaten. After accepting her condolences, I asked her to call me if Velvet showed back up again. That call had come the day before. Marta told me Velvet had moved back in with a new man in tow. She went on to say Velvet had informed her she did not see any reason not to stay there since Thomas's security deposit paid the rent through the end of the month. She told Marta they would probably stay on at least another month or two after that, rent-free due to North Carolina's eviction laws. For an abusive bitch, she certainly knew how to work the system.

I could not believe the gall of this crazy bitch. Just another reason she needed to be taken out. Though I did not have any hard evidence, I *knew* Thomas was not the first man she had used and abused in this manner.

I jumped and emitted a squeak of surprise when a large, dark-skinned hand grabbed the barrel of the rifle, pushing it to point at the ground before jerking the weapon from my hands.

"What the ..." I said as I looked over and up. The moon was positioned behind the man, and because I'd chosen a corner without a working streetlight, I couldn't make out anything about whoever it was, except the hand was large. Extremely large.

"What the *hell* do you think you're doing?" The man growled softly, his voice deep as a well in the Sahara.

Swallowing hard, I set both hands on the open car window ledge before saying, "I want a lawyer."

"Yeah, I bet you do, but you're not going to need one."

"I'm not?"

"No, you're not. Unlock the car and climb out," he ordered, his voice remaining soft.

Without thinking about what I might be getting myself into, I pressed the button to unlock the car and pulled the door latch release. The man outside opened the door, taking my left hand in his.

"Release your seatbelt and climb out."

"Who are you?" I asked even as I followed his directions. When I was standing before him, I looked up, up, up into his eyes. He was at least a foot taller than my five and a half feet.

"Micah sent me," he stated simply. He wrapped his free hand around my upper arm and escorted me around the front of my car.

On the way to the passenger's side, I was able to make out a large, bald, scowling, chocolate-skinned man. I studied his face closely in case I needed to describe it to someone at a later date.

After settling me into the passenger's seat, he cleared the rifle of the five bullets I'd loaded into it earlier. He then worked it further and pulled out the firing mechanism. He pocketed the ammunition and hardware before handing me the weapon.

"Put on your seatbelt," he ordered before closing the door and walking back around the front of the car. He climbed into the driver's seat and muttered a curse. It took him a moment to slide the seat back as far as it would go. Once he was comfortable, he looked at me again.

"Seatbelt."

As before, I moved without thinking of refusing to do as he ordered. I wasn't sure if it was Micah's name, or my lifelong training to do as I was told, but I never considered refusing. As soon as my belt clicked into place, he started the engine and put the car into gear.

He had used Micah's name and had not made any move to harm me, but I still was not sure what to think of this man who had yet to introduce himself. Holding the tight to the barrel of the rifle, I watched the town flash by as he drove straight to my house without needing directions from me. Headlights in the side mirror indicated a car had followed us all the way, even pulling into the driveway. My driver pressed the button on the garage's remote secured to the dashboard before pulling into the garage and parking.

"Cute idea," he said, pointing to the remote.

"Keeps it from getting lost," I answered without thinking.

He nodded, and I thought I saw him smirk at my defensive answer.

It was almost as if he knew everything about me. But how was that? Who was this man and how did he know these details?

Once the engine was off, my driver stared into the rearview mirror for a moment before pressing the button on the remote again to close the garage door. Once it began to rumble down, he opened his door, which released all the locks, and climbed out without another word.

I jumped again when the passenger door opened at the same time. Shifting my gaze, I found myself staring into another stranger's face. This one was a tall, lanky Hispanic man whose hair was combed straight back from his angular face.

"Who are you?" I asked in a high, tight voice. All at once it hit me there were now two strangers inside my house with the garage door down and no way for me to escape.

He did not answer. I waited a moment, hoping he would, but instead, he stepped back far enough to allow me to climb out of the car. The good news was neither man had a gun or knife in sight, and I still had possession of Jarrod's rifle, even if all I could use it for was a baseball bat. Once on my feet, I led the way into the house, very conscious of the two men who followed. Was I willingly walking to my death? Or something worse?

The single light I had left burning in the living room had been joined by the overhead light in the kitchen and another in the guest hall. What was going on?

I heard the sound of pots banging, and water running in the kitchen, but instead of moving in that direction, I headed toward the living room. A woman sat cross-legged at one end of the couch typing fast and furious on a laptop computer. A testosterone-laden movie was playing on the television across the room, though the volume had been turned down so the sound of the crashes and tires squealing was barely audible.

With her long reddish-blonde hair and delicate, lithe figure, my tired mind mused she should have played an elf in the LOTR fantasy movies.

The two men who'd followed me from the garage into the house separated, one going to the kitchen, the other down the hall to the guest rooms. I felt like my house had been invaded, and I didn't know who the invaders were.

"Hello?" I stepped farther into the living room.

"Hello," the woman said, glancing up from the computer though her fingers did not slow.

"Who are you?" I asked again, wondering if she would give me the answer the two men had not.

"Micah," the woman called, looking past me toward the kitchen. "I thought you told her we were coming?"

With a confused frown, I headed to the kitchen. It would have been nice if I had known Micah was returning. I would have cleaned the bathroom and put clean sheets on the guest bed.

"Micah?" I stepped into the kitchen to find him standing at the stove, stirring something in my biggest frying pan.

Instead of appearing guilty for not letting me know he was returning with friends, Micah frowned over his shoulder at me.

I opened my mouth to chastise the man about so many things, when he cut me off. "Samantha, what the fuck were you thinking going after her on your own? You can't be on my team if you're in jail for killing Velvet Flores yourself."

I snapped my mouth shut, opened it, and shut it again, feeling as discombobulated as Dorothy must have felt when she landed in Oz. Shaking my head, I frowned at the man who had returned his attention to whatever he was cooking.

Crossing to his side, I nudged him out of the way.

"What is this?" I asked as a burned, too spicy smell wafted up from the pan which held some sort of tomato and hamburger mixture. My eyes watered as I stirred, and I frowned at the feel of the crust, which had burned to the bottom of the pan.

"Chili," Micah answered as if I were a child and not old enough to be his mother.

"You've burned it and got the spices all wrong, so there's no way it's edible," I said as I picked the frying pan off the stove and carried it out the back door to the porch. I placed the pan on the picnic table to cool and returned to the kitchen.

Micah stood in the middle of the kitchen. "But we're hungry," he protested, sounding like a little boy who had been caught snitching cookies before dinner.

"Give me twenty minutes, during which you can answer my questions," I countered, going to the pantry for spaghetti and sauce. I pulled a bag of meatballs out of the freezer. While I was in there, I pulled out two of the remaining condolence casseroles and put them in the refrigerator to thaw.

Micah huffed a sigh as he moved to the kitchen table and sat down. "All right, what do you want to know?"

"Why are you here? Who are all these people in my house? How did your men know where to find me?" I asked as I filled one of my stockpots with water and set it on the stove.

Before Micah could answer even one of my questions, loud voices came from the living room. "Stay here," he said before rushing out of the kitchen.

I focused on cooking. Twenty minutes later, I carried a large pot of tomato sauce-covered spaghetti into the dining room. Five places had been set at the table with four seats filled with my unexpected guests who watched my every move.

I went back to the kitchen, returning this time with a bowl of meatballs and a plate of garlic toast. Adding them to the middle of the table, I returned to the kitchen one last time for the tray holding five glasses of iced tea. Once I'd handed a glass to each guest, I put the tray on the sideboard, claimed my glass, and settled into the empty seat.

Looking around the table, I met the eyes of each person before waving at the food. "Help yourselves."

Once the dishes began circulating around the table, I turned my gaze on Micah, who sat to my left. "And then I'll want answers."

Micah nodded, but turned his attention to his meal.

It did not take long for the food to disappear, and I was surprised the tiny woman ate nearly as much as the three much bigger men. When the last piece of garlic toast had been torn in half and shared by the two still nameless men, I turned to Micah. "All right, talk."

"You first, Samantha. What were you doing in Velvet's neighborhood with a rifle?" Micah leaned back in his chair and crossed his arms over his impressively muscled chest. The others settled back in their chairs, remaining silent, but watching closely. They all seemed to be waiting for my answers.

"I was going to shoot Velvet," I answered sharply. "Why else would I be in her neighborhood since I don't do drugs?"

Micah exchanged glances with the other people around the table before turning back to me. "Even if you had shot the right woman, you wouldn't gotten out of the neighborhood before all hell broke loose. And even if her friends didn't catch you before you got out of the neighborhood, the cops would have been here first thing in the morning to question you."

"But you said I'd be the least likely suspect." I was confused by the anger I heard in his voice.

Micah took a deep breath and seemed to shift emotional gears, visibly calming. "In a room full of suspects for anyone else's murder, you *would* be the least likely suspect. But if or when Velvet Flores gets hurt or killed, you will be the police's prime suspect."

His answers left me even more confused than ever. "So how do I get my revenge for Thomas's murder? The police aren't doing anything. They've probably closed the case as unsolvable and moved on to something more important like whether glazed or cake donuts are better," I said bitterly.

"You leave Velvet Flores to us," the tiny, still unnamed woman on my right answered. "We're extremely good at what we do, and I see why Micah thinks you'd be the perfect addition to the team. I'm Tia, by the way. Tia Fletcher."

When she reached out with her right hand, I automatically shook it. "Samantha Wycoff."

"Yes, we know," Tia gave a small tinkling giggle that had me smiling in response.

"Yeah, I guess you would," I said before turning my attention to the other two men. "And you are?"

"Grady Alvarez," the Latino man sitting next to Tia answered with a smile.

"Brooklyn Brown," the grumpy mountain of a man sitting on the other side of Micah rumbled.

"This is my team, Samantha. I promise you, Thomas's murder will be avenged, and while you probably will be questioned, you will not have to lie about where you were or what you were doing at the time the bitch dies. But you have to work with us and be patient."

I huffed and looked around the table before focusing once again on Micah. "You should know patience has never been a virtue of mine, but I will try to behave."

"Good girl," Micah said as he patted my hand. "Now, why don't you and Tia go relax in the living room and get better acquainted while we men clean up. Then we're all going to get some sleep. Morning will be soon enough to start your training for the team."

I did a mental count of beds. While I had two guestrooms, the house was still a bed short. "Where is everyone going to sleep?"

Micah smiled. "You don't have to worry about that, Samantha. We'll figure it out. In any case, you won't have to give up your bed."

CHAPTER EIGHT

The Present

"You awake back there?" Brooklyn asked, breaking the heavy silence in the limo as he eased the car into the driveway in front of the three-star hotel I'd checked into earlier in the afternoon.

I jolted back to the present with a gasp. "I'm awake," I responded. I knew he heard the panic in my voice.

I looked at the rearview mirror and met his frowning gaze. "You sure?" he asked, sounding worried and maybe a little amused.

"I'm sure." I nodded as I arched my back and stretched my arms and upper body.

"Okay," he said with a single drop of his head. He climbed out, taking the plastic bag of vomit with him. By the time he rounded the car and opened my door, I had gathered everything belonging to me and that I had touched and was ready to end my second limousine ride. My first one had been from the hotel to the party. Such luxury had never touched this retired schoolteacher before, and I doubted it ever would again. I was grateful for the privilege tonight. Earlier I had felt guilty for such decadence, but at the moment, I was happy I had a driver. I had been able to relax and not have to force inane conversation with a stranger about why I was in town and what I was doing while I was in town.

No one except Micah and Brooklyn needed to know what I was doing in town and why.

As Brooklyn helped me from the car and escorted me across the sidewalk to the front door of the hotel, he said softly, "Micah will meet you in the lobby at eight in the morning for breakfast and help you check out before going sightseeing. You'll head back to New Bern late tomorrow afternoon."

"Got it," I confirmed as I nodded once more. "Thank you."

The big man patted my hand without another word before extricating himself from my hold and heading back to the car. Once inside, I stepped out of the doorway and watched through the window as he drove away.

Once the limo was out of sight, I turned and started across the lobby. Halfway to the elevator, I stopped. I was hungry and was not in the mood to wait the hour or more it would take room service to deliver something from their limited menu. I looked from the elevator to the other side of the lobby where the restaurant and bar were located.

I stood frozen for nearly a minute, debating. My room and room service? Or the bar where I could have food and a stiff drink to settle the after action nerves which were beginning to jangle?

The hungry rumble of my stomach overruled my yen to retreat to my room so I could kick off my shoes. Turning slowly on feet that were screaming for relief, I made my way to the open door of the bar since the restaurant next door was dark. My stomach clenched and my heart began to pick up speed as I stepped through the bar's open doorway.

I was not usually a bar person. I especially was not the sort of woman who went alone into a bar in a strange hotel in a strange city. It was too late to go out and wander the city searching for an all-night diner, so the hotel bar was my best option for hot food.

Glancing around the dark paneled room, I found there were only a half dozen people in the bar, so I had plenty of empty seats to choose from.

I stood in the doorway for another moment, scanning the room before making a snap decision. Turning right, I tried to appear casual as I walked toward the empty table in the back corner of the room. I stepped around the table and sat so my back was to the corner. I couldn't help the sigh of relief that escaped as I kicked off my shoes and wiggled my toes. If I did this again, I would demand to wear flats instead of heels since no one had seen my shoes under the floor-length dress.

I would worry about whether or not I could put them on again later. For now, I needed a drink and some food.

"Good evening," a cute young man dressed in black slacks and vest with a white dress shirt and bright red bow tie said as he approached. "My name is William, and I'll be your server for the evening. What can I get for you this evening?"

"A Jack and ginger ale, please. And do you serve any sort of food?" I didn't care that a lady dressed like me should be ordering a Chardonnay or Pinot wine. I needed a real drink. Over the years, I had found wine would not settle my nerves, and would only result a migraine the next morning.

"Yes, ma'am," he answered politely as he handed me a small folder with the menu. "I'll be right back with your drink."

I nodded absently as I began to peruse the menu. By the time he returned I had decided. "I'd like the sampler platter, please, with ranch, barbecue, and honey mustard sauces."

He blinked in surprise, but nodded with a smile. "I'll bring that right out for you."

I knew ordering a platter would bring criticism and might make me memorable, but I was hungry. If I couldn't finish everything, I'd have them box it up and eat it in the morning.

Meeting Micah in the morning at eight for breakfast was fine, but I normally woke before dawn and needed food and coffee immediately.

I pulled out my phone and checked but had no messages, no texts, nothing to let me know how the other half of this evening's operation was going. That was a good thing, I assured myself. It was still early. It might be a couple more hours, at least, before Tia and Grady moved into action and finished what I could not.

Garner my revenge for Thomas's death.

While I wished I could be there to do the deed myself, it had been repeatedly pointed out over the past six months that when it came to something bad happening to Velvet Flores, I would be the most likely, not least likely, suspect. After all, I had, on numerous occasions, given Sergeant Benson grief about not arresting Velvet for Thomas's murder.

His argument was always the same and made me want to scream. He did not have enough hard evidence to arrest her for anything. And despite Marta reporting to him she had heard Velvet and Thomas arguing before she found Thomas, he was forced to accept Velvet's story that she was fifteen miles away, spending the evening with her mother.

So, while Tia and Grady were in New Bern dealing with Velvet, I was 350 miles away setting another death into play. A death I would never be accused of. A death that would, in fact, not look like a murder.

It had been the perfect solution to my wanting revenge on Velvet, as well as my initiation into the world of "troubleshooting" as Micah called it.

I was surprised the team's handler put his stamp of approval on the Velvet Flores situation, but I had a feeling Micah had done some fancy tap dancing to get him to agree. What he had said did not matter, except he persuaded Mr. Smith to agree. Beyond that, nothing else mattered.

By the time William returned with my platter of finger foods and dips, I had finished my drink.

"Would you like another?" he asked as any good waiter would.

I nodded and handed him the glass.

Only William didn't deliver my second drink.

I had only met Mr. Smith twice before. The first time was during my visit to the area when Micah brought me in to apply for a position with his team. Mr. Smith had worn a silver-gray suit and appeared like your typical forty-something government office wonk. His medium brown hair was short in the classic businessman's style with a glint of silver beginning to show through the strands at his temples. He was clean-shaven and unremarkable in oh so many ways. He was one of those men who could blend into nearly any crowd and be forgotten by dinnertime by anyone who met him.

The only reason I remembered him, was Micah had introduced us, and explained how this man held my future in his hand. Drake Smith was Micah's boss, the team handler, and ultimately, the one who would decide whether I joined the team, or not.

Tonight, Mr. Smith wore a perfectly tailored black tuxedo. His hair was longer than I remembered and the silver maybe a little more evident. His light brown eyes were the same, calculating, judging, making me feel like I was looking into the eyes of a snake while it was trying to decide whether or not to strike. He was the sort of man I was always uncomfortable with because I could not read his bland expression.

He smiled as he set the glass in front of me. He did not wait for permission before pulling out the chair across the table from me and settling into it. He remained silent and watchful as I unrolled the silverware from the deep red cloth napkin and laid the two forks, knife, and spoon neatly to the right of the small plate William had left with the platter.

"I take it you're joining me?" I asked softly.

"I hope you don't mind, but since you're alone, I thought we could talk?" He might have asked a question, I could tell there was no way he would be leaving until he was good and ready.

"I don't mind. Maybe you can keep me from eating this entire platter by myself," I returned.

I picked up the second fork and offered it to him. He took it with the slight smile, which Micah had told me after our first meeting was the most pleasant expression he had ever seen the man show. At anything.

Instead of taking it, he glanced over his shoulder at William. I didn't see what his expression was, but in response, the young man hurried over with a second plate and bundle of silverware.

Once William had drifted away again, I took a moment to study the platter on the table between us. Stuffed mushroom caps, mozzarella sticks, deep fried chicken tenders, stuffed potato skins, bread sticks, and vegetables – baby carrots, strips of bell pepper, cherry tomatoes—were all on display around several small cups of sauces. Nothing unfamiliar, and all things I would normally eat when needing comfort food.

Taking a sip of my fresh drink, I debated where to begin. My stomach clenched in a painful reminder it was empty and did not care what I ate first; I needed to send it food without delay.

Using one of the forks, I carefully put on my plate one of each type of appetizer, as well as one of each of the vegetables to round things out.

Mr. Smith picked up a breadstick and took a bite.

With a deep breath, during which I savored the scents of the food between us, I reminded myself I was a lady wearing a full-on ballgown so I needed to continue acting the part.

Back home, I would have used my fingers to stuff my face, but since I still wore the lace gloves I had worn since arriving to DC to keep from leaving fingerprints anywhere, I traded the fork to my left hand and picked up the knife with my right.

"So, Mr. Smith, what have you been up to this evening?"

I kept my voice soft in the hopes he wouldn't hear the terror shimmering through me like the silver tinsel my mother and I used to put on the Christmas tree when I was a child.

He finished chewing and swallowing the last bite of breadstick before answering. "I wanted to compliment you on a job well done this evening," he said as if he was talking about the weather. "I also wanted to make sure you were all right."

"I'm fine." I answered too quickly before stuffing a mushroom cap into my mouth. It was too hot, and I sucked air and chewed quickly before swallowing, the temperature burning all the way down to my stomach. I washed it down with another sip of my drink, which did little to cool the heat.

Compared to the one I'd eaten earlier, this one was perfect, though a little hot temperature-wise. Flaky crabmeat and breadcrumbs with a cheesy topping and not a drop of vinegar in sight made my stomach rumble with an increased demand for food.

I sat back, having decided I'd wait a few minutes before eating anything else. Mr. Smith continued to study me closely, his expression once again the inscrutable blank slate I had not been able to read at our first two meetings.

"No, you're not. Once Tia and Grady finish their assignment, you'll be better. Or maybe not. In the meantime, I'd like to hear about your plans after tonight."

To most people, his carefully worded statement would be a general inquiry, but from our last meeting, I knew Mr. Smith was never casual about anything. Everything word he spoke had to be dissected for the underlying meaning. But tonight I was not in the mood to parse his words for subtext.

I cut a cheese stick in half, dipped it into the honey mustard sauce, and ate it before answering. "Oh, nothing of any importance. I've started training for my first 5K race on the first of January. Other than continuing training for that, I suppose I'll be singing in the choir for all the holiday services and continue making hats for babies and the homeless. Just boring old lady stuff."

"Oh, Mrs. Wycoff, your life is anything but boring," he said, as he picked up a baby carrot and studied it like it held the answer to world peace. "Since you have a room in this hotel and I don't, why don't you invite me upstairs?"

I blinked at the sudden change of topic. And blinked again when I realized what his intentions were. "No, I don't think so," I responded automatically and without a moment's thought.

I'd been married for decades, and though I had been widowed long enough I knew I should put myself out there and start dating again, I didn't think this man was a good choice for a one-night stand. Even if I were interested in finding a new man, it certainly would not be the man I might or might not yet work for. I only hoped my refusal would not affect my place on the team

Mr. Smith studied me closely as he nibbled on the carrot. Once he swallowed, he smiled again, this time looking like a predator about to take down its prey. As I stared into those light brown eyes, which showed no emotion, I wondered what he was thinking. Would he threaten my life or position on the team for a one-night stand? Or was there something else going on in his mind?

It was then I noticed he rarely blinked.

Would I be taken out because I refused to sleep with the boss?

How would Mr. Smith explain my sudden disappearance from the hotel to Micah and the team?

Would he make a call and cancel the rest of tonight's operation, in which case I would have to pursue my revenge against Velvet Flores on my own?

Or was I making a huge mistake by not saying yes and spending the night with him?

I held my breath as I waited for his next words. It felt like I was nose-to-nose with a copperhead, waiting for it to strike or move on.

And, in the back of my mind, I once again asked myself, "How the hell did I get here?"

CHAPTER NINE

Three months earlier

"Do you realize what you're asking?" the bland, unremarkable-looking man Micah had introduced as Mr. Smith asked Micah. Since the enigmatic Mr. Smith had ignored every answer I had given him since we entered his office, I sat back and pretended to be part of the furniture.

It had taken three months for Micah to decide I was ready to meet his boss. Three months of filling out forms and taking physical exams and strangers in dark gray suits showing up at my front door asking questions. Three months of fighting the growing yen to forget joining Micah's team and hunt down Velvet Flores and put a bullet through her brain. Three months of living my life while waiting for something, anything, to happen, though I had kept busy with training for the 5K and the so-called normal parts of my life.

Three long months.

Finally, the call came from a toneless secretary requesting I present myself to this office today at eleven o'clock. I had driven up this morning, arriving just in time to park my car and walk the two blocks to the door I needed to enter. Along the way, I stopped and bought a hamburger from the street vendor down the block from the front door of this building with a thousand windows and not one sign of which branch of the company or which company the building belonged to. Micah had been waiting, just past the metal detector. He looked dashing in a black suit, white shirt, and blue tie, which matched his eyes. We made our way to the third floor and through the building to this office where I wasn't sure what was going to happen, other than Micah's boss—introduced as Mr. Smith—was not happy.

The office was as bland and nondescript as the man. White walls, industrial gray carpet, with only a desk, a wall unit of file cabinets and shelves, and three chairs as furniture. There was nothing personal about the room, nothing to show this man actually worked here. No family pictures, no knick-knacks, not even any extraneous paperwork lying around. There was a single file on the desk in front of him. I had a strong feeling this was not his office, but an empty one he had procured specifically for this meeting.

Micah studied me for a moment, and I could see the determined glint in his eyes. "Yes, I know what I'm asking. I want to add a new member to my team."

Mr. Smith's expression remained neutral and unreadable even as his cheeks pinked up, a sure sign his blood pressure was on the rise. Jarrod's face used to do the same thing whenever his feathers were ruffled.

"You want to add a widowed, retired schoolteacher with no government, security, *or* military experience to your team. Why? If this is some sort of a joke, it's not funny."

"No joke. Think about it. Samantha is the last person anyone would suspect of being an assassin. Put her in any room, any situation where a dead body is found in the next room, and she would be the least likely suspect. Also, from knowing her most of my life, I can attest to the fact she is one of the most accurate shots I've ever seen, in or out of the military."

I blinked, stunned he remembered. I never told anyone that Jarrod and I used to go shooting at least once a month, and I outshot him every time. When they were little, Jarrod allowed Thomas and Micah to come with us to teach the boys about guns, gun safety, and shooting.

I had only been to a shooting range once since Jarrod's funeral. It was no fun to go alone, and Thomas had always hated the guns, though, as a kid, he went in order to spend time with his father. After Jarrod's funeral, when I asked if he wanted any of his father's guns, Thomas vowed never to touch another weapon, and to my knowledge, he never had.

With that bit of new information, Mr. Smith turned his pale gaze in my direction. "Is he correct? Do you know how to shoot?"

I took a few seconds to consider my answer. "I used to be a decent shot. I've only been shooting once in the past three years, so I'm not sure how good I am nowadays."

Micah patted my arm. "It's like riding a bicycle. We'll have you back to shooting the eyes out of squirrels in no time."

I glanced at him before returning my attention to Mr. Smith. "You shot eyes out of squirrels?" the man asked, sounding shocked.

I shrugged with a smile. "It's the only way to kill the squirrel without ruining the meat. I also used to shoot the heads off doves, too."

I hoped I did not sound like I was bragging, but for some reason I felt the need to put this man in his place.

Mr. Smith did not smile. Micah chuckled.

I met Mr. Smith's eyes squarely as he continued to study me. It was like looking into the eyes of an unknown dog, not sure whether the beast would attack or roll over and ask for belly rubs. I didn't know what he was trying to find, but apparently he found it when he blinked and dropped his gaze.

Glancing at the open folder on the desk in front of him, Mr. Smith nodded and shifted his gaze to Micah. "You have three months to prove her worth. If she can't cut it, she's gone. She'll also have to pass the physical and written tests, the same as any other agent."

My stomach clenched at what he was not saying. I had no idea what he meant when he said I would be "gone" if I could not pass all his challenges. I had a feeling it did not mean I would be sent back to New Bern after promising not to tell anyone about what I had done and seen and learned since Thomas's funeral. After all, I was stumbling around in a world most people did not dream existed outside the pages of crime and political thriller novels.

Micah looked at me and raised an eyebrow in silent query. I nodded. One way or another, I would do this. I could do this.

I would show Mr. Smith, and those he worked for who needed to know, that an over-fifty woman could still offer something to society. As the team's least likely suspect, I could be just as dangerous as Brooklyn and his muscles, or Grady with his knife throwing expertise.

After I dropped my chin an inch, Micah turned to face his boss. "Deal. Three months and not only will she pass the written, physical and shooting tests, she will have aced her first assignment."

Mr. Smith took a breath and nodded, but still appeared reluctant to consider a middle-aged woman for this placement. He picked up the pen on his desk and began to make notes in the file in front of him. As he did, he said, "Three months. Now get out of my office," without looking up again.

Following Micah's lead, I stood and trailed behind him out of the office without another word. Neither of us spoke until we were on the sidewalk outside the building.

"So, what now?" I asked, feeling more nervous now than I did before the meeting, which was saying something.

"Now we get to work, turning you into a super-secret agent woman," Micah linked his arm with mine before starting down the street toward the parking garage where I had left my car.

Not sure I wanted to know how he planned to work that miracle, I kept my mouth shut until we reached my car. Micah took my keys and helped me into the passenger's seat before rounding the back of the car and settling in the driver's seat. Only then did I ask the one question that had been eating at me since I'd woken up that morning. "How does my becoming a member of your team get me revenge on Velvet Flores?"

Instead of answering me, Micah pulled out his phone and made a call.. "I need the team to be taken off rotation for couple of months. No injuries, we'll be training a new team member. Yeah. Okay. Thanks."

He ended the call, opened another app, and his thumbs flew over the screen. Finally, he put his phone away and glanced across the car at me, excitement visible in his expression. "I've got a plan to care of Velvet Flores while at the same time proving to Mr. Smith and the powers that be that you are perfect addition to my team."

I bit the inside of my cheek to stop the flow of questions flashing through my mind. I decided I would take my motherly wait-and-see stance. I knew the answers would come ... eventually.

"Okay. So, where are we going now?"

Instead of answering, Micah started the car and backed out of the parking space. At the checkout gate, he swiped a card through a reader, and the arm lifted. He remained relaxed and in charge as he easily drove away from the nation's capital and headed north into one of the surrounding cities. I was a small-town girl, and the craziness of the traffic we drove through made me so tense I felt like I would shatter into a million pieces. Thank God Micah seemed comfortable driving.

Finally, he turned into a neighborhood and zigzagged for several more blocks before pulling into a wide driveway in front of a square red brick house. It looked like the ones on either side of it, as well as the ones across the street and up and down the street. Minor differences of trim color and yard decorations personalized the houses.

"These houses were built just after the Second World War to help deal with the rapid growth in the area," Micah said as he parked and turned off the engine. "There are such neighborhoods of similar houses all around the area."

He climbed out of the car, and I did the same, still following his lead in this unfamiliar place. He handed me back my car keys before pulling a set of keys from his pocket. Studying his house a moment, I realized it was different than the others. Someone, at some point in the past, had added a wide front porch across the front while the others had an uncovered front stoop at the front door.

Micah strolled to the front door on the right side of the building. He unlocked the deadbolt and doorknob before pushing the door open. He stepped inside and I heard a series of *beeps.* I visualized him disarming a security system before stepping back outside again. Living in the capital and no doubt traveling extensively for his job, I imagined Micah had cameras and recorders and who-knew-what-else as part of his top-flight security system.

"Welcome to my home," Micah reappeared in the doorway and gave me a half bow and sweep of his arm.

I paused a moment before stepping over the threshold, once again feeling like Alice stepping into Wonderland for the first time. How did a government-sanctioned "troubleshooter" live? Would Micah's house be decorated like a dorm room with pinups and porn? Or a military dorm with ammunition and weaponry everywhere?

I held my breath as I took three more steps into the living room before stopping again.

Micah's home was at neither end of the young male decorating spectrum. I felt as if I had entered a home that should be profiled in one of those decorating magazines featuring classic Texas décor. The wide board pine floors shone with a golden glow in the light streaming through the wall of windows that made up the back of the house. The rest of the walls were painted a barely-there peachy-gold color, offering a perfect backdrop for the dark leather couch and a pair of recliners. A natural wood coffee table, matching side tables, and a huge flat screen on the wall finalized the major furnishings. Pictures of exotic faraway places I did not recognize covered the rest of the walls, including the one going up the staircase leading to the second floor.

"It's beautiful," I said, glancing over my shoulder at my host.

Micah shrugged, looking a little flustered. "It's home."

I walked over and began a closer examination of the wall of pictures. "Did you take all these?"

"Yes, ma'am. They're not very good, but they remind me there are still beautiful places in the world."

I didn't want to argue with the man about the quality of his photographic skills, so I rolled my lips over my teeth. The pictures were excellent in color and composition. Each one showcased its subject, usually with an angle or subject I knew would not be on any organized tour I might take. He had been to places in the world I wished to visit, though I was beginning to think it was too late for such adventures.

"What now?" I asked as I drifted around the room, continuing to admire the rest of his artwork on the walls and elsewhere in the room.

"Right now, we'll wait for the team to arrive. Then we'll start making plans for the next three months. I have an idea of what to do, but I need the team to agree to help us before we can move forward," he said as he moved into the kitchen and put on a pot of coffee. "I also need you to commit fully to changing the course of your future, from retired schoolteacher, volunteer, and widowed church lady to that of a government-sanctioned assassin."

He made it sound so easy,

I wished I felt as certain.

Chapter Ten

The Present

"Samantha? Are you still with me?"

My thoughts returned to the present with a bang, and I blinked and realized I had missed whatever Mr. Smith had said. Which might not be the best thing. Especially when dealing with a man who did not want me working for him. He stared at me, concern replacing his usual blank, non-expression.

"Are you all right?" he asked when I didn't respond at once.

I nodded and lifted my glass, only to realize I had finished my second drink. I did not need a third one or I might take Mr. Smith up on his offer to keep me company in my room. Though we were both adults—and from the lack of wedding ring on his finger, I assumed we were both single and available—I could not think of myself having sex with anyone I did not have feelings for. Call me old fashioned, but I had always felt sex should be about more than getting off.

Setting the glass down, I tried to smile. "I'm fine."

His expression did not change, but he also did not inquire further. "How's the training for the 5K going?"

"You know about that?" I asked, shocked he knew anything personal about me.

Mr. Smith gave me a slight smile, which consisted of a rise in one corner of his mouth and a tiny crinkling of the corners of his eyes. It softened his stone-like expression, but not by much. "Samantha, you'd be surprised at how little I don't know about your life. So, how's the training going?"

"I doubt I'll win, but that's not my goal. I just want to finish," I said as

I stared across the room at William. I gave him my "I'm the teacher and I mean business" stare, which not only caught his attention, but had him scurrying over as fast as was dignified in an upscale hotel bar.

"Yes, ma'am," he said with a smile.

"Can you pack this to go and bring me the check, please?" I asked with a smile to counteract the harsh stare of a moment ago.

"Certainly, ma'am." William retrieved the platter I'd barely made a dent in and hurried back across the room to the kitchen.

Mr. Smith didn't say anything. I scanned the bar before returning my attention to him. "You're really not going to invite me upstairs?" he finally asked, looking more than a little surprised.

"I'm really not," I said simply without further explanation.

Appearing as if he wanted to argue, Mr. Smith stood and stepped away from the table. After straightening his jacket, he slipped on his black trench coat. "In that case, I'll say congratulations on successfully completing your first mission. We'll be in touch about your future with Micah's team. Good evening."

A shiver of fear slithered down my spine as he walked away without a backward glance. His final words made me wonder if I'd even be alive to run the New Year's Day 5K.

Before I could freak out about that possibility, William returned with the check and my food packaged in a pretty gold and maroon paper bag. I took a moment to study the bill and silently gasped at the price of the drinks. But since Micah's budget would be reimbursing me for everything, I simply shrugged. I added a substantial tip and signed the ticket, charging everything to my room. Another bit of proof I was not in New Bern on this particular night.

I stood and slipped my cloak back on before picking up the bag and leaving the bar. The alcohol and small amount of food I'd eaten had settled the adrenaline surging through my system earlier, but Mr. Smith had done little to relax me. Now all I wanted was a shower and some sleep.

I hoped the bed was comfortable. It did not even occur to me as I walked across the lobby in my stockings.

"Miss? Miss!" a voice called behind me as I hit the elevator call button.

I did not turn around to see who was shouting or why. I thought I was the only one in the lobby, but still jumped when a hand patted my arm. Whirling, I found William standing behind me, smiling broadly.

"You forgot your shoes, ma'am," he said, holding up the shoes I had completely forgotten about. Only then did the chill of the tile floor sink in.

"Oh, my, thank you," I gave a small laugh. "I can't believe I walked off without them."

William merely smiled as he handed over the shoes. "You'd be surprised how many women do the same thing."

"Well, thanks again," I said as the elevator doors opened.

"Have a good evening, ma'am," he winked before turning away.

It took a second for the meaning of the wink to occur to me. He obviously thought I was headed upstairs for a tryst with Mr. Smith. Tempted to call him back and assure him I was not, I shrugged and stepped into the waiting elevator.

I smiled. Let him think what he would. If questioned, he could share the gossip and gift me with a reputation I could never earn on my own.

With a small giggle, I pushed the button to my floor with the heel of one shoe. As the doors closed, I scanned the lobby, but there was no one watching me, so I allowed myself to relax against the side wall of the elevator and slipped my shoes back on. I winced and blinked back tears as I put down each foot. A moment later, the elevator slowed and stopped. I counted to four before the doors parted, allowing me to exit. I looked around the gray-walled, maroon carpeted foyer area and sighed to find myself alone. Mr. Smith was not waiting for me. Then I tried to remember which way led to my room.

Checking the numbers and arrows on the wall, I started the long, slow trek down the hall to my room at the far end of the building. By the time I reached my room for the night, I swore I would throw all my high-heeled shoes away and only buy pretty comfortable flats from now on. I stepped into my room and flipped both locks before kicking off my shoes once again.

"Don't take anything else off unless you mean it," a familiar bass voice said from deeper in the room. "Or should I leave quietly and come back in the morning?"

"Micah?"

I took the time to slip off my cloak and hang it up on the padded hanger it had arrived on before walking the rest of the way down the short hallway between the bathroom on one side and the closet on the other. I stopped once I could see the entire main room. Micah stood to my left in the small area between the bathroom wall and the bed.

"What are you doing here?"

Micah sidestepped down the narrow space, stopped beside me, and looked from me to the hall door. "No company?"

I chuckled as I crossed to my suitcase. Pulling out the ragged comfort pajamas I'd brought, I asked, "What is it with men thinking I'm going to sleep around tonight?"

Micah blinked, frowned, and shrugged. "It's what I did after my first five missions. Got drunk and slept with a woman I'd picked up in the hotel bar. Who else...?"

"I stopped at the bar for dinner and a drink. Mr. Smith joined me and strongly hinted I should invite him up here to"— I used air quotes before continuing— "talk. But there's no way I would sleep with him, even if he weren't the boss."

Micah gave me a look that was part disbelief and part anger with a smidge of jealousy thrown in, though I did not understand why. Was he jealous?

"What?" I asked. Once again I felt like I was trying to maintain my footing on two balance balls.

"Smith was in the bar and said you should invite him up here?" Micah asked with a frown.

I nodded. "He suggested I invite him up to talk, but yes, it seemed like he expected me to sleep with him. Did I mess up by refusing? Because frankly, the man doesn't do a thing for me."

Micah released his breath in a whoosh before smiling. "No. You just proved to him you're more of a lady than he's been giving you credit for. If he tries anything else, let me know, and I'll deal with him."

"Wonderful. Thank you. Now it's time for you to get out," I said with a smile as I pointed to the hall door.

Micah remained where he was, ignoring my not-so-subtle hint. "What are you planning to do now?"

"I'm going to take a shower and wash off the two pounds of makeup and hair crap that stylist you took me too insisted I needed in order to fit in with high society. Then I'm turning on a mindless old movie and attacking the appetizer platter I did not feel comfortable inhaling in front of Mr. Smith. I'm also hoping to receive notification that Tia and Grady finished their half of the mission. Once I know vengeance has been dealt to the bitch-who-shall-not-be-named, I'm going to curl up in the middle of this wonderful bed and sleep until my six-thirty wake-up call."

I pushed Micah backward toward the hallway door. I knew he allowed me to bully him. If he had not wanted to go, I knew he would still be standing where he had begun. He must have seen something in my expression that allayed whatever fears he had. "Now go away, and I'll meet you in the lobby at eight in the morning."

"I'll go, but if you need me, I can be back here in twenty minutes," Micah offered as he flipped open the locks and pulled open the door. "Don't be afraid to call, whatever the time."

"Thanks for the offer, but I'll be fine," I said even as I nodded my agreement.

Micah stepped into the hall without any further encouragement from me.

"Good night, Micah."

I watched the door close behind him and pushed it the last few inches until it clicked, and I secured both locks. Checking through the peephole, I watched as Micah stood in front of my door, typing on his phone screen for a minute before pocketing the phone.

He stared directly at the peephole, as if he knew I was still standing on the other side. "Good night, Samantha." With a sigh, he turned and disappeared from view. I trusted he would go home and get some sleep himself.

It took less than a minute to strip off the dress and underthings. The stockings went into the trash, and I hung the dress up. The underthings went into the dirty clothes bag in my suitcase.

Once I was in the shower, I adjusted the water to as hot as I could stand it, then adjusted the spray until the water pulsed out. Turning around, I sighed as the pulsating water beat on my shoulders and upper back. Once those knots eased, I took my time washing my face, hair and body while working to ignore the falling tears as I fully crashed from the adrenaline storm from earlier.

When I finally turned the shower off, I felt lighter and had cleared the guilt and other dark emotions from my psyche. After combing and drying my hair, I dressed in the flannel pajamas I'd brought with me. I took a few minutes to rearrange my suitcase, pulling out what I planned to wear in the morning and packing up everything else except the ballgown and cloak. After a stop at the small refrigerator for the bottle of soda I had brought with me from home, I settled on the bed with the takeout bag for a middle of the night picnic.

I grabbed the remote and flipped through the channels until I found one of my favorite old romantic comedies playing. I turned the volume up enough so I could hear it, but not enough it would bother the neighbors. I sat in the middle of the bed cross-legged as I opened the bag from the bar and pulled out the contents. The routine of spreading the food across the bed in front of me helped me finish the shift from Mama Sam, superspy sniper woman back to Samantha Wycoff, retired schoolteacher. William had packed each food separately and added several good sized cups of the dipping sauces as well as extra napkins and a plastic packet containing a plastic fork and knife.

"Thank you, William," I murmured with deep appreciation.

I opened the food packets and dove in. My earlier hunger, which had fled during my unplanned meeting with Mr. Smith, returned with a vengeance. The alcohol I had drunk had kicked while I was in the shower, leaving me feeling strangely relaxed as I started eating. I rotated foods and savored every bite, not allowing myself to think of the hundreds and hundreds of calories I was consuming. Tonight, calories did not count.

I also tried to keep my mind blank, but the movie, which had always been one of my favorites, was not able to hold my attention. My thoughts once again started down the road of "Is this really the life I want?"

CHAPTER ELEVEN

The Past

"You can't be the one who kills Velvet Flores."

Those were the last words I expected out of Micah's mouth once the team had gathered and settled around his dining room table. We had coffee in front of us and a box of cookies in the middle of the table. Tia and I sat on one side of the table, which would seat six. Micah sat across from us with Grady and Brooklyn at either end.

I stared at him, not sure I had heard his words correctly.

"What do you mean, I can't kill Velvet Flores? You're the one who agreed to help me get revenge on the woman. You told me about the other men she's hurt or worse, and the many, many other bad things she's done. She's a killer. She's not going to change, and the world won't miss another monster like her. Why can't I just walk up to her and put a bullet in her brain? It's what she deserves."

Micah shook his head. "While everything you say is true, and Velvet Flores is a bad, bad woman, you can't be the one to walk up and put a bullet in her brain. She's the one person in the world where you would be the prime suspect instead of the woman least likely to be responsible."

I opened my mouth to argue, but Tia chimed in first. "He's right, Mama Sam. No matter when or where or how that bitch dies, once her body is found, you'll be questioned about your alibi. There's no way you can be anywhere within a hundred miles of her when she goes down. But don't worry, she will go down. You will get your revenge for your son's death."

Grady and Brooklyn remained silent, but nodded their agreement.

I knew I was out of my depth talking about cold bloodedly killing this crazy bitch, and I understood they were right, but my still grieving heart and soul screamed for justice.

"So she's going to get away with it? I can't kill her without the police coming after me, and the police have given up investigating her, so she's going to get away with killing Thomas?"

Hearing myself, I sounded like a grumpy five-year-old who needed a nap.

"No, she won't get away with it. But you won't be the one to do the deed. You'll be far away from New Bern when she dies so when the police show up at your door and question you, you'll be able to honestly say you were out of town, and they will believe you," Micah said as he stared deep into my eyes. "In the meantime, we are keeping an eye on her while we build a strong enough case we can take to Smith who has the authority and clout to order her extermination. Right now, we have to focus on something else. We have three months to turn Samantha Wycoff from a retired schoolteacher slash church lady and semi-professional volunteer into an agent qualified to be the team's newest sharpshooter."

"She's taking Fitch's place?" Grady sounded more than a little surprised at the announcement.

"That's the plan. I also want her able to work up close and personal in case she ever needs to. She'll be the last one suspected of any dirty deed, but this morning, Smith declared she has to pass *all* tests to become an agent. Written, physical, and weapons."

They looked troubled, but the others nodded their understanding.

"What if she doesn't?" Tia gave voice to the question that had been on my mind since our meeting with Mr. Smith.

"She's gone," Micah answered, his voice flat and devoid of emotion.

The others gasped, and all eyes turned in my direction. I met each set of eyes for a moment, hoping my expression was reassuring. By their continued shocked expressions, I knew I had failed.

I turned to Micah before I asked, "Smith meant I'm dead, didn't he? If I don't pass all the tests and join your team, he'll have me killed, right?"

Micah took a slow, deep breath before dropping his chin once in an affirmative motion. "Yes. You'll be an agent or you'll be eliminated as you will have learned too much to allow you to walk around untethered."

"But that's not going to happen. We have three months to get you in shape and trained in the ways of Micah's Misfits," Tia said. She reached over and laid her hand on my fingers, which were twisted together on the table in front of me.

"Micah's Misfits?"

"That's Smith's pet name for us. We were all about to be fired, or worse, for a variety of reasons when Micah brought us together and forged us into a team. It took a couple of missions, but now we're considered the baddest of the bad asses the government refuses to acknowledge," Grady explained with a grin, which sent a shiver of nervousness through me. That was the most the man had ever said in his smoke and whiskey roughened voice.

I mulled over this new information before I smiled. While retribution for Thomas's death remained my top priority, my focus began shift. I wanted to do this, to become a part of this team, to help them do what legal channels could not. I wanted to help bring the monsters of the world to a kind of justice they deserved.

Rising, I went to my purse on the table nearest the door and pulled out the empty journal and pen I never went anywhere without. I smiled at the cover embossed with the words that seemed so appropriate today. "When you fall, as you inevitably will, rise and burn brighter for you are the hottest badass in the universe."

Returning to the table, I opened the journal to a clean page. "I guess we'd better get started if we're going to turn me into one of the baddest of the bad in only three months."

That moment was the turning point for me. That was the second I *knew* my life would go on with renewed purpose. I would not be returning to the river and thoughts of suicide again any time soon. At least as long as I focused on training and becoming a Misfit, I would not feel the need to swim the Neuse River to my death any time soon.

I needed to do this for Thomas, not only to obtain the revenge I so desperately wanted, but I needed to do it for me. I needed to be more than simply Samantha Wycoff, widow, retired schoolteacher, church lady, volunteer.

Even if no one but the four people at this table, and Mr. Smith, knew of my involvement in their dark practices, when my life eventually did end, at least I would know I had made a difference in ways much bigger than making hats for charities, working on the church's newsletter, and singing in the church choir.

By the time the sun set and we went out to a neighborhood Chinese restaurant for dinner, the next three months of my life had been sketched out and calls made to line up private instructors for the skills I needed to learn. Once we finished, the saké began to flow, and things got a little fuzzy as the team shared stories of their exploits as a way to indoctrinate me into their ranks.

§ § §

I woke the next morning with the hangover from hell. Opening my eyes a millimeter at a time, I slowly looked around but did not recognize the room I found myself in. The floor was a golden hardwood and the walls were painted white with plain navy curtains as their only decorations. The furniture consisted of a full-size bed, a generic four-drawer dresser made of unfinished pine, and a wooden chair I vaguely recognized as belonging to Micah's dining room set. The carryall I had left in the car with a change of clothes sat on the dresser.

I eased myself into a sitting position, breathing shallowly as the pounding in my head worsened and my stomach rolled. Closing my eyes, I sat for a few minutes, praying I did not get sick all over the floor.

"Note to self," I whispered, "never, ever again try to keep up when drinking with the team."

Once my stomach settled slightly, I pushed slowly to my feet. I took two steps and found myself leaning against the dresser as the room shifted and rolled under my feet like a rocking boat.

Glancing down, I realized I was still wearing the clothes I had worn the day before. They were wrinkled from being slept in, and I really wanted a shower. First, I needed to confirm I was at Micah's house. I combed my fingers through my hair, trying to put some order to it, moaning as the hairs pulled at my scalp, adding to my pain.

Opening the door to the hall, I found the bathroom and used the facilities before heading downstairs. I also took two ibuprofen capsules with a swallow of lukewarm coffee in a mug sitting the counter by the sink. Pouring the rest of the coffee down the drain, I rinsed out the mug, and filled it with cold water, which I drank without pause. Filling the mug a second time, I carried it with me as I headed downstairs.

Micah was sitting at the dining room table, reading something on his tablet. "Morning, Samantha."

"Shhhh," I hissed. "Too loud."

He smiled as he pushed from his seat and headed into the kitchen. "Sit down and I'll get you some breakfast."

"Not yet," I whimpered. "Maybe later."

Micah returned to the dining room, and stopped behind me. He gently massaged my temples with two fingers. The scent of peppermint filled the air around us. Between his oily massage, the painkillers, and the water I continued sipping, the headache abated, leaving me feeling as limp and washed out as an ancient t-shirt.

"Remind me to volunteer to be designated driver next time," I said once I felt relatively normal.

"Sure thing. I'll let you be the responsible adult next time," Micah sounded entirely too cheerful for so early in the morning. "Just don't get between Brooklyn and Grady if they get to arguing while they're drunk."

CHAPTER TWELVE

"Are you sure we're headed in the right direction?" I asked the few days later as I drove deeper and deeper into the eastern North Carolina wilderness. Having spent most of my time running up and down highway 70, I had a hard time believing people actually lived out here, an hour from New Bern and well off any beaten path I knew of.

Micah checked his phone, swore softly, and turned it off, before leaning over the center console so he could see the odometer. "No cell signal. From the directions Jax gave me the turn should be about another mile up this road on the right."

I continued driving, wondering if we would be hearing banjos or seeing Bigfoot or some other swamp monster before we arrived.

Slowing for another curve in the road, I kept my speed slow as we approached yet another turn a few dozen yards further.

"There it is." Micah pointed to a six-foot tall red and gold banner next to what could be kindly described as a dirt path leading into woods so thick I could not see anything but bushes and trees.

I reluctantly turned and took my foot off the gas, allowing the car to roll at its own pace down the rough road. "Next time we'll bring your SUV," I said.

"I offered, but you wanted your car," Micah reminded me.

"Only because I had already packed my weapons and range bags in it."

"Yes, ma'am," Micah responded with a definite smirk in his voice.

Yes, I had demanded to take my car and not because I did not want to transfer six guns and my range bags to his SUV. I needed to feel the control having my own car gave me.

Before anything further was said, the road emerged from the forest into a large clearing. The road passed a 19th century white two-story farmhouse, one of several designs prevalent in the area. Beyond the farmhouse, the road ended in a parking lot with several pickups and SUVs. I pulled in and parked before taking a steadying breath.

"We'll go check in and see if Jax is here before getting the gear and heading to the range."

I nodded and reached for my purse sitting on the floor behind the passenger's seat.

"You won't need that. Just take your wallet and keys," Micah said.

Without a word, I reached into my purse and pulled out my wallet. Taking the keys out of the ignition, I waited until Micah was outside the car before climbing out and pressing the automatic lock.

As we walked toward the gray metal building, which housed the business side of the range, Micah looked at my wallet and chuckled. "We need to get you a new wallet. A small and discreet one that will fit in your pocket."

I studied the bright purple clutch-style wallet that held money, checkbook, and a dozen credit cards and was nearly as big as a purse. "You don't like my wallet?"

"How are you going to hold a rifle and your wallet at the same time?"

I shrugged. "I'll figure something out. Maybe you can hold it for me while I shoot."

Micah was still laughing at the suggestion when we entered the building. Glancing around, it appeared this was a combination gun store, weapon supply store, snack shop, and office.

"Go ahead and look around, I'll be with you in a minute," the older woman instructed as she rang up a pair of men who had the haircuts, build, and wary stances of war weary Marines.

Before I could take three steps, a man stepped out of the doorway under the "Office" sign. "Hey, Kerrick. Great to see you."

As he crossed to exchange a manly, back-thumping hug with Micah, I took a moment to study him.

Tall and gangly, with a pale, freckled face, bright ginger hair pulled into a short queue, and a long, full beard covering the lower half of his face and neck, he reminded me of a redheaded Smurf. He wore work boots, jeans, and a T-shirt with the logo of Sanitary Fish Market and

Restaurant, an Atlantic Beach restaurant and one of Jarrod's favorite places for seafood.

Once they finished their greeting, the two men turned to me. "Jax Marcum, this is Samantha Wycoff, your student. She was quite the shot when I was growing up but hasn't touched a weapon in several years. I need her sharpshooter-ready by Thanksgiving."

Jax nodded as he looked me up and down. "Miz Wycoff," he said extending his right hand.

I shook it with a nervous smile. "Call me Sam."

"Sam. Welcome. Have you filled out paperwork yet?"

After filling out liability release paperwork, registration forms, and setting up a membership for the private shooting club, I paid for several targets. Instead of retrieving the weapons, Jax walked us out to the range, and gave us what sounded like a well-rehearsed speech, covering basic safety and security rules of the range.

Once he finished, Jax made a note on my paperwork and glanced to Micah. "Where do you want to start?"

"Handguns and long range weapons," Micah said.

Jax nodded. "All right then. What is she shooting?"

§ § §

By the time we climbed back into the car, I was hot and tired. My arm muscles and back were sore, letting me know I would be sore for at least a day or two. I also felt about twenty pounds lighter and more confident than I had in years. We had blown through several boxes of ammunition, but by the time Jax's next student arrived, it only took a few minutes to recall everything Jarrod had taught me.

"She's good," Jax said as he and Micah carried the four rifles and two range bags with the handguns, cleaning supplies and ammunition we had not shot to the car. I followed, my arms crossed so I could rub the muscles of both upper arms at the same time.

"Yes, she is," Micah agreed.

"I was better five years ago," I refuted.

"And you will be again. Today wasn't about making you feel bad, Sam; it was about seeing what we needed to do to get you back to shooting the eyes out of squirrels and heads off doves," Jax said.

I looked at Micah in shock. "You told him about that?"

"I wanted him to know he wasn't dealing with a complete newbie," Micah answered defensively. "And from what I saw today, it won't be too long before you're that good again. And that kind of accuracy will be what the evaluators are expecting."

I blinked as it hit me those targets I was shooting at would eventually be live bodies.

"I'd like to meet with you once a week. How about Thursday mornings?" Jax said as I pressed the button to open the trunk and the men loaded the weapons cases.

I took a moment to think about my schedule. "Thursday mornings will work. What time?"

§ § §

My upper arm muscles were still sore from the morning at the shooting range two days later when Grady put me in his pickup truck and we drove out of New Bern, turning onto a road I knew led nowhere. It ended in a circle with two driveways, though you could not see either house from the road. Grady turned down the road to the left and drove until we reached the plantation house overlooking the Trent River.

"Welcome to my studio," the tall, muscular man gave me a half bow. "I am Maleko Devey."

I was not sure what intrigued me most. How a man with what sounded like an upper crust British accent ended up living in coastal North Carolina in a historically registered plantation house, or his appearance.

From my shorter vantage point, he seemed as big and burly as Brooklyn. I spent a moment wondering who would win if the two men brawled. Maleko was dressed in black leggings and a white t-shirt that lovingly outlined the rippling muscles of his upper body. The sleeves had been cut off to accommodate the bulging muscles of his upper arms. His creamy brown skin reminded me of the café au lait I had enjoyed during my book club meeting the evening before.

It was not until he turned to lead the way from the front door deeper into the house that I saw his hair. The sides had been shaved, leaving the top strip long. It reminded me of the Mohawk style, which had been popular decades ago, with a twist. The hair down the center of his head was long enough he had braided it in a narrow version of a French braid, which went down the back of his skull with the braid ending at his shoulder blades.

I glanced over my shoulder at Grady and raised one eyebrow in query at this British Samoan hippie. He lifted one shoulder in a shrug but didn't speak.

"We'll work in here today," Maleko said as we entered what would have been the grand hall or ballroom. It had been turned into a gym of sorts, with a weight set in one corner, a boxing heavy bag and treadmill in another. The rest of the room had thick pads on the hardwood floors, no doubt so he didn't hurt his clients while he threw them around.

At the doorway, he toed off his bright purple Crocs and walked barefoot down the three steps and into the two-story tall room. I followed his example, thankful Grady had convinced me to wear clogs and not sneakers. My T-shirt and yoga pants, worn over a new sports bra, which compressed everything so it didn't jiggle, seemed appropriate clothing in this space.

It had been years since I'd been to a gym or organized exercise class, and knew I was sadly out of shape. Yes, I was now fast-walking three miles every day as the first step to running the 5K in a few months, but that was far from being ready to throw down with someone like Maleko.

"Today I'm going to take you through a series of exercises to evaluate where we need to focus our attentions, okay?" Maleko had reached the middle of the room and turned to face me.

I looked around, but Grady had disappeared. A moment later, he walked back into view, carrying a well-stuffed wingback chair, which he placed in the doorway before he sat down and pulled out his phone.

"Samantha, I need your attention here, please," Maleko said.

"I'm so sorry." I turned my head so fast I heard my neck crack.

"That's all right. But for the next hour, I need your attention on me and not that slugabout," Maleko said with a grin.

"Hey, be nice," Grady called without lifting his eyes from his phone's screen. "I'm here as backup or in case you need a test dummy."

Maleko grinned and winked at me. "Well, a dummy at least."

That earned a growl from Grady, but no further argument.

"All right, Samantha, let's get to work."

Over the next hour, Maleko had me bend and stretch and work muscles I did not know even existed. He had me walk on the treadmill, lift weights, and then put boxing gloves on me and had me hitting the heavy bag.

By the time Maleko called an end to our first training session, I was one hot, sweaty body ache. Everything hurt from my eyebrows to my toes. Slipping my feet into the clogs, I leaned against the wall as Maleko and Grady talked just out of earshot. A couple of minutes later, Maleko walked away, and Grady joined me in the doorway.

"Here, take these," Grady handed me a packet of over-the-counter pain pills before twisting the top off a bottle of water. I popped the tablets and drank down half the bottle without taking a breath.

"Thanks."

Grady nodded before leading the way back through the house to the front door where Maleko rejoined us.

"You're going to need these." Maleko handed me a large bottle of a creamy substance and a DVD case. "A rubdown with this lotion at night, after your shower, and again in the morning, if you need it, will help with the pain. We're going to have to meet three days a week instead of two. On the days you don't come here, I want you to do at least one of the videos on this DVD to work on flexibility. You also need to start alternating running and walking. Ten steps each to begin with, and increase at least two steps running every four days."

I accepted the bottle and DVD case with a tired smile. "Thanks."

"Don't worry, Samantha, we'll have you beating up Grady and Micah in no time," Maleko assured me with a confident smile.

"Uh-huh," I replied skeptically. As tired and sore as I felt following Grady to his truck, I was not so certain.

In fact, I was pretty sure I would never, ever be in good enough condition to pass whatever physical tests Mr. Smith would require for me to join the team.

Chapter Thirteen

It took nearly two weeks before my body stopped hurting after every workout with Maleko. Acetaminophen and ibuprofen and Maleko's magical minty scented lotion became my best friends. I would have quit after the third day if it had not been for Micah and Grady who worked out with me. They made it seem so easy, and I felt more and more like a bumbling elephant beside them. I kept a picture of Thomas sitting by the television to remind myself why I was doing this.

After about ten days, my muscles stopped complaining over every move. I also noticed I was standing taller and my flexibility was increasing.

It was then Maleko started the next phase of my training – street fighting. We started with the basics, and my instructor was impressed at how quickly I picked everything up.

The classes with Jax and Maleko, in addition to my weekly church choir rehearsals, my monthly book club meeting, and the weekly Tuesday evening grief support group Becca convinced me to join, kept me busy. The rest of my days were spent learning the bookwork I needed to pass the agency's written test.

I was so busy I forgot about the river. I wanted to visit the duplex Thomas had rented and smash Velvet Flores' face in. I fought the urge, and only drove by the house once a week while I was running errands. I did not stop, did not get out of the car, but I kept an eye on the house just the same.

As the weeks passed, I adapted and my skills grew exponentially. In addition to sharpening my distance shooting, Jax helped me perfect my marksmanship on every weapon he and I had access to. By our eighth week together, Jax declared I was more than ready for my marksmanship test. He told Micah that, for a civilian, I was a better shot than most Marines he had taught. I took his words as a high compliment from the otherwise taciturn man.

Maleko was equally impressed with my progress. After two months, I faced Grady and Brooklyn on the mat. The challenge was to stay on my feet while defending myself against the two men who were better trained and had a lifetime more experience at street fighting. Micah and Tia sat on the ballroom steps, watching as I walked to the center of the mat with Grady. I think I shocked us all when he came at me and I put him on the mat with two moves before doing the same with Brooklyn who was twice my weight and all muscle.

"Yay, Samantha! You showed them who the mama bear is," Tia said, loudly applauding as Brooklyn and Grady pushed themselves off the mat.

The book learning was the easiest part of my training, thanks to my near photographic memory. I read through the book of the agent's training twice and knew the material. Determination to join Micah's team helped me complete six months of class work in only two months.

§ § §

On the third of December, my cellphone rang late in the evening. As a woman on my own, I did not normally answer the phone if the screen did not show a name from my contacts list, or if the call came from a number I did not recognize. Checking the screen, the area code showed the call was coming from Washington DC, so I felt I had better answer. If it was a spam call, I could always hang up and block the number.

"Hello?" I answered hesitantly, half expecting a recorded spam call of some kind.

"Ms. Wycoff, this is Drake Smith."

My stomach immediately knotted when the team's handler identified himself. His voice on the phone was as bland as everything else about the man.

Something was off. Way off.

I took a breath and reminded myself to be polite as my heartbeat picked up speed. Why was the team handler calling me at this time at night? Had something happened to Micah and the team, who had visited for Thanksgiving, but gone home a few days after.

"Good evening, Mr. Smith." I did not say anything further and forced myself to wait. It felt like I was staring down a snake, waiting to see if it would strike or slither away.

"Ms. Wycoff, I'd like you to come to my office for a meeting tomorrow morning at eleven. Please bring gym clothes with you and plan to spend a day or two in the city." As usual, Mr. Smith was efficient when making his demands.

"Yes, sir," I replied automatically. "Can you tell me what this meeting is about?"

"Your evaluation, Ms. Wycoff. I have an upcoming operation you would be perfect for, but first, you need to pass your evaluation. There is also paperwork that needs to be completed regarding payment for your training time and future services."

"All right, I'll be there," I did not understand why this call had come from Mr. Smith and not Micah in his capacity as my team leader.

Unless Mr. Smith had plans for me that did not involve Micah or the team?

After confirming the time and place of our meeting, I hung up. I was not surprised he gave me a different office number than our first meeting. I stared at the phone as I took long, slow breaths to try and calm my jangling nerves. Something about this made my gut knot with how off it felt. Over the years, I had learned to trust my gut about people as well as situations I walked into. The more I thought about Mr. Smith's call, the more wrong this all felt.

Stroking a finger across the phone's screen, I speed dialed the man I now saw as not only as a second son, but also my mentor and boss.

"Samantha? What's wrong?" he answered on the first ring. I heard jazz music in the background and wondered if I'd interrupted something.

"I'm sorry for calling so late. I was wondering if you would mind having a houseguest tomorrow night and maybe one or two more? Mr. Smith just called and wants me to report to his office tomorrow morning for my evaluation," I reported succinctly.

I had learned Micah, as well as the rest of the Misfits, did not do small talk and though well versed in technology, they really did not trust it enough to have phone calls which lasted for more than a very few minutes.

He muttered a string of words I did not understand but had heard him say before. I knew they were a curse of some sort in a foreign language, but I was not exactly sure which one. One day I would ask him to translate, but tonight was not that time.

He went silent for a moment, and I did not say anything to break the silence. I knew he was evaluating what I had told him and was making plans on how to deal with this twist.

"Okay, we'll do like last time. I'll meet you inside the metal detectors at the office at ten-thirty and we'll go from there."

I nodded. "Sounds like a plan. See you tomorrow morning."

"Samantha," Micah said, sounding deadly serious. "You're ready for this. Know that. Confidence in yourself and your training is half the battle. If you go in knowing you're ready, you'll knock his socks off. And I'll be there to back you up every step of the way."

And with those words, everything in me that had tensed up suddenly relaxed.

"Thanks, Micah. I'll see you tomorrow," I hung up before he could say anything further.

Going to the pantry, I studied at the large wall calendar containing my secret schedule. The next three days were free of training sessions, but there was an extra choir rehearsal for the Christmas cantata I would miss. The choir would have to get along without me for one practice.

This trip was more important.

CHAPTER FOURTEEN

When I walked through the front door of the no-name government building at ten-forty the next morning, I found not only Micah waiting, but the entire team. The men were dressed in black suits, white shirts, and black ties. Only their shoes differed. Micah wore dress shoes while Grady wore what looked like highly polished biker boots and Brooklyn wore black sneakers. Tia wore a black dress with a dark gray jacket over it, no doubt to hide the numerous weapons she carried with her at all times. With it, she wore black hose and mid-heel black ankle boots. They looked like they were going to court ... or a funeral.

I wore black dress pants with a dark gray cashmere sweater set and black dress boots under my long black wool coat. I carried a large carryall over one shoulder, which held my purse as well as my gym clothes and sneakers. I left the handgun I had begun carrying the last couple of months locked in the glove compartment of my car, which was parked in the garage two blocks away.

"Don't you all clean up well," I said with an approving smile as I approached after clearing security.

"Thanks." Micah grinned as he stepped up and gave me a hug.

Grady and Brooklyn shifted as if uneasy with the praise even if it was just about their clothing.

Tia stepped forward and gave me a quick hug. When she stepped back, we circled up. "We talked and decided we all needed to be here to back you up," Micah said softly. "We need you for your cooking skills, if nothing else."

I chuckled as the others nodded their agreement. Micah took my hand and placed it on his arm.

"Ever the gentleman," I murmured as he patted my ice-cold fingers, which held tight to keep from running back the way I had come.

"Hey, we can be gentlemen, too," Grady protested as they fell into line behind us.

"Sure you can," Tia said, her skepticism clear in her tone.

Brooklyn merely grunted.

It took us longer to get to Mr. Smith's office than I remembered from our last visit. Then I recalled he was not in the same office. When we left the elevator on the fourth floor, I took over leading the way. I stopped when we reached room B428, needing a moment to breathe before throwing myself into whatever Mr. Smith planned for my day.

"You're going to be great," Micah said softly.

The others murmured their agreement and patted my shoulders.

I took a deep breath, lifted my head, and straightened my shoulders. Turning to face the foursome, I smiled. "Thank you. No matter which way today goes, thank you for your help, your friendship, your confidence in me. And if I fail, and Mr. Smith decides to have me disappeared, promise me"—I shifted my gaze to stare deep into Micah's eyes—"promise me you'll find Velvet Flores and make her pay for what she did to Thomas."

Micah nodded and, without saying a word, lifted his right hand, curled his fingers into his palm before placing our hands over his heart.

I glanced at the others and they, too, held their fists over their hearts, each making a solemn vow to exact my revenge if Mr. Smith ended my career with the team before it had even begun.

Blinking back the tears filling my eyes, I nodded. "Thank you," I whispered.

Before I allowed my emotions to overwhelm me, I checked my watch. 10:57. Time to face my future. I turned and opened the door and stepped into room B428. The air moving across the back of my neck told me Micah and his team of misfits had followed me into the room.

The room was not an office like the one where Micah and I had met Mr. Smith before. This was a conference room with a table that would easily seat a dozen or more people. Mr. Smith sat at the far end with two other men in dark suits sitting on either side of him.

The three men stood as I walked in.

"What's this?" Mr. Smith said when he saw Micah and the rest of the team enter.

"You requested a member of my team appear before you without notifying me," Micah answered from where he stood behind my left shoulder.

"And how do you know that?"

I cleared my throat before answering. "Because I called him. I thought it odd you would contact me directly, instead of going through my team leader."

"Uh-huh, except you are not officially a member of Micah's team yet, Ms. Wycoff," Mr. Smith said before sitting. "Well, let's get started. You have a busy day ahead of you. The sooner we get started, the sooner you'll be able to return to North Carolina. The rest of you may leave; we have no need of you at this time."

Though he did not say so outright, it was clear Mr. Smith did not approve of my actions or the team's presence in what was no doubt a meeting meant to knock me off-balance.

All at once, it hit me. Mr. Smith did not want me as a part of Micah's team. He did not want me under his supervision at all. And without saying so outright, he was determined to find a way to keep me from joining the team and from gaining my revenge.

"No, I don't think so," Micah said as he and the team moved to sit in four of the empty chairs at the near end of the table. "We're here to support our teammate. We won't interfere with the evaluation, but we will be here for Samantha."

Mr. Smith's face turned red, and for a moment, it seemed as if his head was about to explode. It took a moment before he finally released an explosive breath of air. "Fine, but the first one to speak or take any action to help her, she's gone. Do you understand?"

A shiver of trepidation raced down my spine as the four exchanged a glance. Brooklyn, Grady, and Tia nodded before Micah said, "Agreed."

I smirked as the four pulled out their phones and settled in.

Mr. Smith turned his full attention to me. "Ms. Wycoff, we'll begin with the written test, before moving to the gym for the physical portion of the evaluation. Is that acceptable to you?"

I took a breath and shrugged. "That's fine."

I was really glad I had stopped on my way into town and eaten a burger when I filled up with gas. Otherwise, my stomach would be protesting the day's agenda.

The man to Mr. Smith's right picked up a computer tablet from the table in front of him and carried it to me. After turning it on, he cued it up. When a hand appeared on the screen, he took my right hand and placed it against the glass. Several seconds later, a green light moved up and down before the screen changed and he lifted my hand.

"You have two hours." His voice was as bland and unemotional as his expression.

I nodded and glanced at my wristwatch, noting the time. I turned my attention to the screen. Closing my eyes, I took several deep breaths to center myself before I began reading the directions. Taking a breath, I blocked out the rest of the people in the room. I had always been a good test taker, and didn't expect this to be any different.

It only took ninety-six minutes for me to finish the test. When I pressed the completed button, the screen went blank for several seconds. I'd begun to wonder if the tablet had died when a new screen appeared showing I'd passed with a score of 96 percent. Before I could throw up my hands and do a chair dance, three dings sounded at the far end of the table. Mr. Smith and his cohorts checked the screens of their phones

"Congratulations, Ms. Wycoff," Mr. Smith said, his tone slightly disappointed. "You passed the written portion with flying colors. Now, we'll move on to the physical portion of the evaluation."

"Thank you," I responded without looking at Micah or the others.

"The next portion will take place in the gym in the basement. I know you'll want to change clothes, so we'll reconvene in Gym B in thirty minutes."

§ § §

By the time I followed Micah and the rest of the team out of the building, it was nearly dark. People were flooding the streets as they left their workday behind and headed home. I was hungry, sore, and exhausted. While Micah and the team were proud of me, I wasn't so sure. Mr. Smith and the two men he had never bothered to introduce had not seemed impressed by my street fighting abilities.

While I had been slammed to the ground a time or two, it had not stopped me. I was able to hold my own against the three men Mr. Smith brought in to test everything I had learned over the last ten weeks. After my hand-to-hand skills had been proven, we moved on to the shooting range next to the gym. I efficiently proved my marksmanship skills with every weapon they handed to me.

When it was all done, Mr. Smith and his cohorts simply nodded and walked away without comment. I wasn't sure whether I should leave now and go home or wait for his decree.

I jolted when Brooklyn stepped up beside me and dropped a thick, muscular arm over my shoulders. "You did good, Mama Sam. I think you might have even scared Smith by how well you did."

I tilted my head and looked up at the man who stood a foot taller than me. While I felt old and still out of shape, despite losing a good twenty pounds, he was all thick bones and muscles and had just said more words than I'd ever heard him say at one time. Micah had told me he was a man of action, not words.

"Thanks, Brooklyn," I said as we reached the parking lot. "You going to ride with me?"

The big man chuckled as he shook his head. "Nah, I won't fit in your itty bitty car. I got my ride. Grady rode with me, so we'll meet, get the beer, and meet you at Micah's. We gotta celebrate."

I would have preferred to wait until Mr. Smith made his final decision about whether I would be joining the team or not, but Brooklyn was right. Even if the team's handler had not been impressed by my actions, I had passed every test they'd thrown at me.

It *was* time to celebrate and be proud of all I had accomplished over the last two and a half months.

And even if Mr. Smith refused to make me part of Micah's team, I knew I was good enough and now had the scary mad skills to take Velvet Flores out myself.

Of course, getting rid of her body was another thing.

Chapter Fifteen

"No, you are not going to kill Velvet Flores," Micah stated later that evening, in a steel-laced tone which told me he meant business. After the team split up to pick up takeout and beer, we gathered again at Micah's house.

"But she needs to die," I stated once again.

We had been arguing this back and forth for the last twenty minutes, and we were both nearing the end of our patience.

I would be heading home and returning to my life in the morning. If we ever finished this discussion.

Until now, no one had brought up Velvet Flores' fate. I finally did, and this argument had been going on between me and Micah for much longer than necessary. There was no resolution, or end in sight. Micah was determined to protect me, and I was just as determined to deal with the woman who had caused my son's death.

"How about this, Mama Sam: You *cannot* be the one to kill Velvet Flores," Tia said, sounding much too calm. "When she shows up dead, and she will, you will be the first person the police question. You need to be far, far away from New Bern when the bitch dies, and have easily provable proof for plausible deniability."

"But I want her dead," I grumped, my tone now one of a whining child and not a woman who was two decades older than anyone else in the room.

"And she will be. Thomas's death will be avenged," Micah assured me in a suddenly softer and calmer voice. "But *you* can't be the one to administer this act of revenge. The only way to keep you out of jail and on the team is for you to be out of town while it's happening. So you, me, and Brooklyn will be working your first mission as part of the team while Tia and Grady deal with Velvet Flores. Not only will you have justice for Thomas, Mr. Smith will have proof you're ready for future fieldwork."

I mulled over their words for a moment. They were right. As much as I wanted to be standing over her, watching the life flow out of Velvet Flores, I agreed I could not be there. Not if I wanted to stay out of the New Bern jail and off the NBPD radar.

Taking a deep breath, I held it while I counted to ten before releasing it on a sigh and nodding. "All right, I give. I won't be the one to deal with Velvet Flores."

The tension in the room dissipated, and everyone around the table relaxed.

"With that, we'll be going," Grady said as he and Tia stood and headed to the pile of coats on the staircase inside the front door. In less than a minute, they were gone.

"But I wanted to know how they're going to do it." I said as the door closed behind Grady.

"No. The less you know about what they'll be doing, the better. You can't even know when it's going to happen, much less how they're going to deal with her. That way, when the police come to question you, you can honestly say you know nothing about it," Micah explained, his voice now softened to one of the understanding man who had come to the wake and offered me a way to earn retribution for my son's death all those months ago.

Micah pulled a plain manila folder out of the cabinet behind him and handed it to me. "While they take a little trip to North Carolina and deal with your problem child, we will be dealing with this man. Read the file and then we'll talk."

As I read the contents of the folder I realized there were people in the world so much worse than Velvet Flores. I had a feeling her history of abusing people, taking and/or selling drugs, and whatever else she might have been into was worse than I suspected, or even what Thomas had known, but that was all right too. I didn't need to know. After doing an in-depth study of her, the team agreed she was worthy of their type of extreme and definitive vengeance, and that was that.

I read the report in the folder and only had to run to the kitchen to throw up in the sink once as I flipped through the color pictures of some of the target's known victims. But I didn't stop. I forced myself to continue until I had read every word and seen every picture. I would probably have nightmares for weeks, but wasn't that part of the job too?

"This is one of those men," I murmured once I had studied every page. I carefully straightened the papers and placed them neatly in the file before closing it and sliding it to the middle of the table.

"One of what men?" Brooklyn asked, his voice a deep rumble.

I looked from him to Micah and back again. I had both men's full attention. "One of those men who deserve to be assassinated. One of those men the courts release because the judge or jury decides they are too successful, or too white, or too whatever to go to jail. One of those men who raise their sons to be just like them, to think they can get away with anything because they'll get a slap on the wrist *if* they get caught and actually go before a judge. The ones who buy off witnesses or threaten witnesses and get away with it," I said, amazed at the bitterness in my tone. "The ones who'll never spend more than a few hours in jail because they've got the legal system wired in their favor. After Thomas died, I started a list of those people. The ones who deserve vigilante justice since the legal system is broken and the rich white men who are running the country don't care."

Both men nodded their agreement. "Yes, this man needs to go on your list. In fact, he goes to the top of it. He is going to be your first kill. The challenge is he cannot die on US soil. And it cannot appear like someone in the United States government, killed him. Which is where we come in. He'll die by our hand and the"—Micah used air quotes, which seemed odd for such a manly man—"official government can deny knowing anything about it."

I nodded, although I couldn't see how we would take out such an evil man while keeping the government out of it. "So how do we do this?"

"We use futuristic nanobots contained within a virus which—to the world in general—doesn't exist, a rifle Congress outlawed in 1988 before it was ever fully functionally invented, and your newly refined sniper skills. You will be the least likely suspect in a room full of movers and shakers at a party when the man is shot. He won't die until he leaves the United States and returns home. It doesn't matter if it's in a week or month. His death will appear like a heart attack. With his health history and Russian politics and healthcare, we're hoping an autopsy won't be ordered. Everyone will likely believe his heart simply gave out."

I considered his words as I stared at the folder on the table between us. Finally, I lifted my gaze to meet Micah's. "I'm in. What do we do now?"

Chapter Sixteen

The Present

I was at the hotel's front desk the next day, arranging to stay another night when Micah walked into the lobby. After the clerk assured me I could keep the room for several nights if I wished, I turned to Micah.

"Good morning," I forced a smile, despite feeling both mentally and physically exhausted.

I'd only gotten a couple hours of sleep, which was one of several reasons I decided to stay another night. I also hoped to do some Christmas shopping and clothes shopping for warmer winter clothes since I was in a shopper's Mecca. All I had to do was convince Micah to change the day's itinerary a bit.

"Did you sleep at all?" Micah asked as he leaned in and brushed a kiss on my cheek.

He looked nearly as tired as I felt. I didn't ask if he had gotten drunk and laid once he'd left the party. Micah's sex life was none of my business and I really, *really* wanted to keep it that way.

"A couple hours. I never sleep well the first night in a different bed. I also don't sleep well my first night at home after a trip," I said with a smile. "I decided to stay another night in hopes of sleeping better, and I'll go home in the morning."

Micah nodded without comment, though I could see he wanted to say something. He held out his arm instead. "Shall we go? Brooklyn's waiting, and that boy gets grumpy when he's hungry."

Having never seen Brooklyn when he was not in some kind of a grumpy mood, I could not imagine what he would be like if he was truly hungry. I had a feeling people might get hurt, or worse.

"Well, we'd better hurry then." I took Micah's arm and allowed him to guide me out the front door to where his deep red muscle car waited. It wasn't until we were pulling into the parking lot of the restaurant that it hit me.

Staring across the front seat, I blurted out, "This is about more than just Thomas's death, isn't it?"

I met Micah's stunned gaze calmly, squarely, despite my insides shaking like trees in a hurricane.

How had I missed that small detail? How had I missed that this was not a one-time thing? How had I gone from a church mouse slash semi-professional volunteer to an assassin wannabe?

Oh, yeah.

My son had been brutally murdered, and I wanted revenge.

But I also needed something more in my life. Something to fill my days and give me a reason to get out of bed in the morning.

Was being one of Micah's Misfits that something?

Micah blinked at my question before smiling. "Yes, Samantha, this is about more than getting revenge for Thomas. I'm not exactly sure what Smith's problem is with you, except he's been trying to find a reason to break up my team since we were assigned to him. I'm hoping you'll come to work with us and have a long and happy next career as a ghost. I know it's not as exciting as, say, being a professional volunteer for the church, but I can assure you that we take care of business and save lives with what we do, even though we hope no one will ever know of our involvement. Of your involvement."

He took a breath and turned his attention back to driving. "You've passed all your evaluations and successfully completed your first mission. You've proven your worth to me and the team. Now it's time for you to decide whether or not you want to continue walking on the dark side of life as one of Micah's Misfits or return to your quiet life in New Bern."

He paused for several long seconds. When I did not respond because I was not sure what to say, he began again, this time softer and with a sad tinge to his voice. "He called me, you know. About a year ago. He made me promise that if anything ever happened to him, would I take care of you.

"Of course I said yes. You were like a second mother to me, and he was the brother I never had. I never thought it would happen, that he would die first. In my career, I always knew I would die early, even took the most dangerous assignments when no one else wanted them. When Thomas called, I knew it was time to stop taking chances. You became my reason to be safer and take fewer risks. And now Thomas is dead."

"And you're saddled with me," I said as I blinked back tears, not sure if this was a good thing or a bad one.

Micah turned to look at me, a sheen of tears in his own eyes. Then he blinked, and they were gone. He smiled. "No. Not saddled. I was gifted with you. Now, enough sad talk. Let's go have breakfast and spend the day sightseeing. Whatever you want to do."

"Even if it's shopping for Christmas and warm clothes?"

"Yes, even shopping. Maybe you can help me with gifts for the team."

I nodded my agreement, and we left the conversation in the car. As Micah had told me before, the decision was up to me. I had to figure out if this new life was the one I wanted or not.

As we crossed the parking lot, Micah's phone sounded the alarm, signaling one of his team was calling.

After checking the screen, he swiped to answer. "Kendrick."

He listened for nearly a minute before saying, "Got it. Thanks," and ending the call.

He pocketed his phone, but did not say what the call was about. I had a strong feeling it had to do with the end of Velvet Flores.

"It's done, isn't it?" I asked, my stomach knotting in anticipation.

"I can't tell you that," he said. "You need plausible deniability when the cops show up on your doorstep about an hour after you get home."

Looking deep in his eyes, I saw the truth.

Velvet Flores was dead.

Taking a deep breath, I nodded. "Thank you, Micah."

After stepping close and brushing a kiss on his cheek, I took his hand and dragged him toward the restaurant door.

All of the sudden, I was starving.

§§§

I arrived home early the next afternoon and pulled into the garage when a dark gray sedan arrived and parked so it blocked my driveway. A moment later, a white New Bern Police Department SUV pulled around the sedan and parked in front of it at the curb in front of my house.

I parked and left the garage door open so they could see what I was doing as I unloaded. I popped the trunk and began pulling out my suitcase and the shopping bags packed in there. Not only had I finished my Christmas shopping for the few people I had left to buy for, but I had also bought myself a number of heavy winter sweaters and a new winter coat that would be warmer than what any of the stores in New Bern offered. I piled everything by the garage door leading into the kitchen while a policeman and another man ambled up the driveway.

I recognized the uniformed officer as Sergeant Benson from six months earlier so I focused on him. The other man, who was a good ten years younger than the sergeant, wore jeans, a yellow button-down shirt, an ugly teal and orange tie, and dark suit jacket with scuffed up black biker boots. Whoever he was, his appearance did not impress me.

"Hello, Sergeant Benson," I said with a hesitant smile. "What can I do for you today? Have you finally caught Thomas's killer?"

Instead of allowing Sergeant Benson to answer, the other man pulled out a notebook. "Missus Wycoff, where were you yesterday morning between two and seven o'clock?"

I fought back a smile at his flat "Joe Friday" vocal impression, which I had to admit was surprisingly good. Instead, I focused on his rude behavior. He was an ass, and I decided to teach him a lesson about dealing with the public. I was, after all, a retired schoolteacher.

"And you are?" I asked in my most haughty Southern matron tone.

I might have been raised all over the country, but we had lived in New Bern long enough for me to pick up the customs and attitudes of the Southern mama bear. Rudeness was not only *not* tolerated by the Southern mamas, it was called out and corrected on the spot.

The man blinked and blinked again, apparently shocked I did not immediately cower and answer his accusatory question. He swallowed hard and took a breath before answering, "I'm Detective Sotal, ma'am."

He opened his mouth again, probably to repeat his question. Before he could, I shifted to stand squarely on both feet before crossing my arms over my chest. Raising one eyebrow and trying not to smirk at the man, I asked, "You're not from around here are you?"

I saw Sergeant Benson take a step back, as if he knew what was coming and did not want to be hit with body parts as I taught the detective a lesson in manners..

Somehow, my questions flipped the young detective completely off his game. "No, ma'am, I'm not."

"Well, *Mister* Sotal," I emphasized the word mister, "Here in the South, we treat people with courtesy. All people. Which means we introduce ourselves and allow for a moment of pleasantries before delving hip deep into business. We also allow others to answer the questions asked of them instead of steamrolling over the conversation."

"Yes, ma'am," the detective blinked and looked younger and more embarrassed by the minute. I would bet my entire new winter wardrobe this was not the first time he had been called out on his behavior. Maybe, this time, he would take the lesson to heart.

I turned my attention back to a broadly grinning Sergeant Benson who appeared to be fighting to keep from laughing hard and long. I smiled sweetly and said, "So, Sergeant Benson, what can I do for you today?"

It took the uniformed man a moment to swallow down his mirth and get himself under control. His voice sounded choked when he finally replied. "Well, Miz Wycoff, there's been a development in your son's case. We're here to ask where you were yesterday morning."

With a smile, I waved toward the garage. The bags still sitting in the trunk and the ones piled by the door were clearly visible. "As you can see, I've been out of town shopping. Why? What's going on?"

"*Where* were you shopping, Missus Wycoff?" Detective Sotal asked. "What city? What state?"

Taking a breath and huffing it out on a sigh, I turned face to the man. "I was in northern Virginia and Washington, DC doing some last minute shopping both for Christmas as well as to stock up on some warmer clothes for winter," I explained, my tone chilling at the detective interrupting once again. "Can *you* tell me what's going on, Detective, since you are apparently incapable of allowing Sergeant Benson to answer my questions?"

The man again hesitated, and I could see his frustration building as he began to clench and unclench his hands. When the detective looked at Sergeant Benson and gave him a stiff nod, I had to bite the inside of my cheek to keep my chuckles inside. If nothing else came from this meeting, maybe Detective Sotal would have learned some common courtesy, Southern style.

"Miz Wycoff, Velvet Flores was left on the front steps of the police station just before dawn yesterday morning. She'd been beaten so severely, she died on the way to the hospital," Sergeant Benson said.

"Did she say I hurt her?"

Sergeant Benson shifted, looking extremely uncomfortable at my blunt question. "No, ma'am, she never regained consciousness before she died. But after your quite vocal accusations since your son's death, you are a possible suspect."

"Ma'am, do you have receipts, from a hotel or restaurant or something to prove how long you were in Virginia?" Detective Sotal broke in.

I blinked. "You don't believe me?"

"Ma'am, we have a dead woman about whom you verbalized threats to a police officer not so very long ago," Detective Sotal said. "We would be remiss if we did not ask for receipts to prove you were not in the area as you claim."

Forcing myself not to get more offended by his skepticism, I nodded with a sigh. "Yes, I have receipts. I just need to get my purse."

Rounding the car to the passenger's door, I felt the two men follow me into the garage. While Sergeant Benson remained relaxed and at ease, the detective rested his hand on the butt of his gun.

I opened the passenger door, reached inside and pulled out my carryall. After closing the door, I carried it around and set it on the hood of the car. I opened the bag and dug into the big side pocket where I'd tucked the receipts so they would all be in the same place.

Pulling out the bunch, I thrust them toward to Detective Sotal. "There you go, Detective. Receipts for gas, the hotel where I stayed, and the shopping. Satisfied? I was three hundred and fifty miles away for the past three days."

The man took the papers from me and slowly, deliberately, flipped through them. He took his time to check the time and date stamps on every single slip of paper. Finally, he handed the stack back.

"Thank you, Missus Wycoff. If we have any further questions, we'll be in touch," he turned and stalked to his car.

"He is an ass," I said to Sergeant Benson as I tucked the receipts back into my bag.

"Yes, he is. But they say he's very good at his job," Sergeant Benson answered. "If you know of anyone who might have done this, please let us know."

Sergeant Benson offered me his business card before following the detective out of my garage and down the driveway. As the two men stood between the two cars and conferred for several minutes, I finished unloading the trunk, the back seat, and finally the front seat. Once everything was piled by the door to the house, I closed up the car and pressed the button on the wall by the light switch, activating the garage door. It rolled down, securing me the garage, and by extension, the house.

I did not take an easy breath until the door stopped moving. Then I took a deep breath, held it for a count of five before slowly releasing it again as I worked to relax.

Though Velvet Flores's death was not a surprise, the manner of her death was. And to know Grady and Tia were responsible for the woman's demise made the reality of the dark world I had voluntarily entered hit home.

Hard.

All at once, my stomach rolled over and all the bad for me snacks I had nibbled on during the drive home began to bubble up.

I dropped the bags and packages on the garage floor, fumbled through the keys on my ring, then unlocked the door. Leaving the bags behind, I hurried inside and raced to the nearest sink. I ended up puking my guts out in the kitchen sink as I realized I was no longer the naïve church lady who knit for charity and donated her time wherever I could.

I was now responsible for two people's deaths. I had taken a life in revenge for Thomas's life, forgetting that vengeance belonged to God, not to man.

My stomach finally empty, I rinsed my mouth and cleaned the sink.

Heading back to the garage, I transferred everything into the house, and spent the next hour unpacking and putting everything away. The gifts went to the dining room to be wrapped. The new clothes went to the laundry room to be washed. The black party dress and cloak were folded up to be taken to the cleaners.

Finally, I put away the empty suitcase and curled up on my bed, where exhaustion, both physical and mental, overwhelmed me.

I knew the police would return with more questions, but for now, I would have a private little party because the crazy bitch who had beaten Thomas had suffered the same fate as he had. I knew it was un-Christian to celebrate, but I couldn't help myself. Revenge had been achieved, and I hoped I was no longer at the top of their suspect list.

The team's crisscross plan had apparently worked.

Chapter Seventeen

The Present

Minutes before dawn on Christmas morning, I drove through the cemetery gates and made my way around to where my family lay buried. Taking the red and white roses I'd bought the night before with me, I made my way through the field of headstones to the one Jarrod and I had chosen together. We'd bought a plot on the back edge of the cemetery and had gotten another double plot for Thomas. He had been between girlfriends and had vowed not to ever marry, but we had remained hopeful that one day he would change his mind.

Standing in the grass beside where I knew Jarrod's casket lay, I couldn't help the tears filling my eyes and rolling down my cheeks. "Merry Christmas, my love. I know you've been worried about me, but I'm doing fine. Micah Kerrick helped me find a new purpose in life beyond singing in choir and knitting hats. We are working for the government, bringing bad guys to justice in rather unconventional ways. I love you and still miss you so very much."

I laid half the roses in my arm at the base of the headstone, under Jarrod's name. Then I stepped over to where Thomas lay on the other side of the piece of real estate where someday I would rest for eternity.

"Merry Christmas, baby boy," I said as my voice broke and tears rolled freely down my face. "I'm sorry I could not talk you into getting away from that woman, but I want you to know she's in hell where she belongs and will never hurt anyone else. I did not do it myself, but the police came to me a few days ago and told me she'd been killed in a manner similar to how you had been beaten. Only she didn't make it to the hospital. Micah is keeping the promise he made to you. He's talked me into going to work with him. From what he's told me, I'll be doing all the traveling I talked about doing since your father died.

"Oh, and with Micah's help, I'll be running the New Year's 5K next week. I'm not hoping to win, just finish. Maybe next year I'll try to place in the top three. For now, I need to get home because Micah and his team showed up last night to share Christmas with me, and I have to make breakfast. I love you, Thomas, and I want you to know I will eventually join you, but right now, I'm where I need to be here on Earth."

Laying the rest of the roses on his grave at the base of his headstone, I turned and made my way back to the car. It took a few minutes to stop crying so I could drive, but I was soon on my way home. I needed to get there because I'd promised the team the same Christmas breakfast feast I had always cooked for Jarrod and Thomas. They had shown up yesterday afternoon in Brooklyn's SUV, claiming we were now a family and families spent holidays together.

They even brought the still-wrapped gifts I had left with Micah for them. I was so happy to see them, I burst into tears. My plan for today, since I did not have any family to celebrate with, had originally been to hide from the world with a stack of DVDs and every comfort food I had laid in during an impromptu shopping spree the day before.

The team had hit the grocery store on their way to my house, and picked up enough food for a month. Since I could not sleep, I had gotten up around three and put together a couple of breakfast casseroles before coming to the cemetery. Once I returned home, I would put my efforts and attentions into cooking and caring for these four people who were now my family.

I had not heard from Mr. Smith since our meeting at the hotel after my first assignment, and I was beginning to worry about whether or not I would survive the holiday season. But for today, I would put aside everything except the happiness of having a new family to focus on, and a new direction for the future to look forward to.

§ § §

A week later, less than a minute after I crossed the finish line, my phone rang with the distinctive tone Micah had assigned to his phone number. It sounded more like an air raid siren than a simple ring tone, which compelled me to pull it out of my pocket and answer immediately.

"Hello?" I panted.

"Just received word Mission 5K was a success," Micah said by way of greeting. "Are you okay? You sound out of breath."

"I finished, so I guess that means it was successful," I bragged as I walked away from the crowd of runners and their supporters.

I had no one waiting for me at the finish line, and while I had not been one of the last runners to arrive, I was far from the front of the pack. But I had finished the race. I was proud of myself for not chickening out and for actually participating. I earned the pin or badge or whatever the plastic participant's bag I had been handed as I crossed the finish line held.

"Congratulations on finishing. Next year, I expect you to place top three in your age group," Micah said.

As I ran through town, I thought I had seen Tia and Grady along the race route, but that couldn't be. Could it? After we had spent a wonderful Christmas Day together, we had dropped Brooklyn and Grady at the airport after dinner. They had an assignment, and the company plane was to fly them there and back. The next morning, Tia and Micah had taken Brooklyn's SUV back to Northern Virginia. Micah had left me on my front doorstep with a bear hug and the warning he or Mr. Smith would be in touch, but in the meantime, I should return to living my life as normal.

I had laughed and asked what normal was, because the life I now lived, with weekly shooting lessons and self-defense classes was far from what had been normal eight months before.

We answered my question in unison, "Normal is just a setting on the dryer," and then laughed together.

As I crossed the parking lot toward my car, I was stunned to see three men standing shoulder-to-shoulder and leaning against my car. Micah still held his phone held to his ear as he grinned at me.

I ended the call and pocketed my phone as I hurried as fast as my sore legs could carry me across the distance between us. "What are you doing here?" I asked. I stepped toward Brooklyn first.

"Congratulations," Brooklyn rumbled softly in my ear as he gently hugged me.

Mr. Smith stepped up next. He appeared uncomfortable as he took my hand and shook it. "Congratulations. On the race and your excellent scores on your evaluations. I also wanted to apologize. I was way out of line at our last meeting. I'm sorry if I embarrassed you. You have proven yourself a valuable member of the team, and I hope you continue to be."

"Thank you," I said, pulling my hand away as soon as politely possible.

I turned to Micah who pulled me in for a hug.

"Speaking of work, we're hoping you're up for a little trip."

"Are you sure?"

All three men nodded in unison. "We don't have a lot of time, so what do you say?" Micah asked.

I thought about what I had planned, for the next couple of weeks, which was nothing I could not miss. A couple of phone calls and I would be free of my obligations to the church choir and monthly book club.

At the thought of once again being a vital part of this team of secret superheroes no one would ever know about, my heart began to pick up speed. I hesitated only another moment before smiling. "Do I have time to take a shower and change clothes before we have to leave?"

Micah nodded with another wide smile that made him look like a cover model. "Tia and Grady are meeting us at the house. We've got about two hours before we need to be on the plane."

The End

About the Author

Cooper McKenzie always thought she had been born a hundred years too late, though she appreciates air conditioning, computers, and other conveniences of modern-day life. She lives in central Texas with her mixed breed companion, Honey, the Princess Fuzzybutt.

For all titles by Cooper McKenzie, please visit

www.coopermckenzieauthor.com

www.ingramcontent.com/pod-product-compliance
Lightning Source LLC
Chambersburg PA
CBHW070941250626
47159CB00009B/3334